THE LAST
GOOD MAN

THE LAST GOOD MAN

Daniel Lyons

The University of Massachusetts Press

AMHERST

This book is the winner of the Associated Writing Programs 1992 Award in Short Fiction. AWP is a national, nonprofit organization dedicated to serving American letters, writers, and programs of writing. AWP's headquarters are at Old Dominion University, Norfolk, Virginia.

Printed in the United States of America
LC 93-3464
ISBN 0-87023-865-5 (cloth); 978-3 (pbk.)
Set in Adobe Minion by Keystone Typesetting, Inc.
Printed and bound by Thomson-Shore, Inc.

Library of Congress Cataloging-in-Publication Data
Lyons, Daniel, 1960–
The last good man / Daniel Lyons.
p. cm.
ISBN 0-87023-865-5 (alk. paper).—
ISBN 0-87023-978-3 (pbk. alk. paper)
I. Title.
PS3562.Y4483L3 1993
813'.54—dc20 93-3464
CIP

British Library Cataloguing in Publication data are available.

Some of the stories in this collection have appeared elsewhere, sometimes under different titles and in different form: "The First Snow" in *Story;* "Violet" in *Redbook;* "The Greyhound" in *Playboy;* "The Clear Blue" in *Santa Monica Review;* "The Birthday Cake" in *Crescent Review;* "The Last Good Man" in *GQ;* "Brothers" in *Oxford American.* "New Math" was part of a manuscript for which the author received a Hopwood Award at the University of Michigan. "The Greyhound" was awarded first prize in the *Playboy* College Fiction contest (1992).

For Rosamund,
and in memory of my mother

In a dark time, the eye begins to see

THEODORE ROETHKE

Contents

THE LAST
GOOD MAN

The First Snow

THE NEWSPAPER prints their names, and I admit that makes it worse. There are sixteen of them, and my father, whose name begins with A, is at the top of the list: Henry Abbott.

There was a rest area in Derry, apparently, and a path into the woods, and a giant hollow sycamore in the meeting place where they were arrested. The story in the *Gazette* says New Hampshire state troopers have been watching for weeks, camouflaged. They have videotapes.

The phone calls begin: more words for *fag* than I knew existed. Mom takes a call, listens, and slams down the phone. Her hair is matted to her head, her blouse is wrinkled, her eyes are bloodshot from not sleeping: she looks the way she did the time Jenny's appendix burst and we sat up all night in the hospital waiting room. She unplugs the phone.

"Visiting his mother," she says, disgusted. That was the excuse Dad used when he went out yesterday. I'm trying to remember how long he's been visiting Nana on Sundays.

She lights a cigarette and then stubs it out, so hard that it snaps. "Bob, I'm sorry," she tells me, "but I won't live with this."

Dad spent the night in jail. Mom said she couldn't handle the police station, all the smirks and snickers. He was arraigned this

1

morning, and now, six hours later, he's still at his lawyer's office. I imagine this is a first for Mr. Pangione. He's a contract man: wills, taxes, divorce—the last, I think, may be of use when the criminal case is finished. I picture the two of them in their big leather chairs: Mr. Pangione embarrassed and looking down at his desk, my father fidgeting, afraid to go home.

Dad does more than jump into strange cars in rest areas. The big surprise is that he has a steady. All I can gather from the conversation taking place behind the bedroom door upstairs is that the steady is married, and that he too is shocked about Dad's adventures in the woods.

"What, and do you love him? Do you love him? I can't believe I'm asking this! My husband! I'm going to be sick."

Dad starts to cry. I can hear his wet words, but I can't make them out. Oddly, the news of the steady doesn't seem so bad.

Jenny and Nelson are in the family room playing Chutes and Ladders, oblivious. Jenny is seven and Nelson is five—both, I hope, too young to remember this. I, however, am seventeen.

I spread the *Gazette* out on the kitchen table and read the list of names again, wondering which one was the one with my father. What an image: all those men, moving silently in the woods, my father among them.

I fold the paper and put it up on top of the refrigerator, where Jenny and Nelson won't find it. I think about stupid things: Should I still do my homework? Will we have Thanksgiving? What are we doing for dinner tonight?

Mom solves the last one: Kentucky Fried Chicken. We sit, the five of us, at what I suppose will be our own Last Supper. Jenny and Nelson make castles with their mashed potatoes and Mom doesn't scold them; Dad grips the drumstick Mom gave him—at least she's got her sense of humor—and makes fake small talk about school, where he did not teach today; Mom gives him polite fake responses between gulps from her tumbler of gin; I watch for a while, then stare straight into my plate, not wanting to meet any of their eyes.

Later, Mom packs suitcases and duffel bags and moves with Jenny and Nelson to the Driscolls' house. I tell her I'm going to stay at home.

Mom puts the kids in the car, then comes in to ask me once more to come with her. For a moment I am literally standing between them: Mom at the open door, angry; Dad by the fireplace, drumming his fingers on the mantel, looking away. He is a schoolteacher, a man accustomed to dignity, which he is now working hard to maintain.

"Well?" she says.

The fact is, I feel bad for my father. I'm not going to leave him here alone.

"You go on without me," I say.

Just like any other night, Dad sits slack-gutted in his recliner in the family room, watching television. I go in and sit on the couch. The show is NFL highlights.

"Look at that hit," he says. "Jesus Christ."

There is a slow-motion replay: the arms stretching for the pass, the safety spearing in from behind, the tiny moment when there is no motion, then the legs lifting up, the head snapping back like a car crash dummy's, the ball tumbling free.

"Jesus Christ," he says again. He grabs a handful of peanuts from the can, shakes them in his hand like dice, and looks at me. "You going to stay for the game?" he says.

The air in the room feels overpressurized, like in a submarine that has surfaced too quickly.

"I don't know," I say.

"Well," he says, smiling, "I'm glad you decided to stay."

Suddenly I want to reach over and smack him for being so happy; I'd like to wipe that smile off his face.

"I'm glad you're in such a good mood," I say.

He sits up and says, "Bob, look—"

But I turn my back. I mumble something about homework and run upstairs to my room.

I'm on the phone with Drew—yes, everyone knows; some jerk has already started a joke—when another call comes in. It's Mr. Ryan, Dad's principal. I click back to Drew, tell him I've got to go, then call down to Dad.

"Well, I don't need to go to school tomorrow," he says when he arrives upstairs a few minutes later.

He tries to smile, then stands slope-shouldered in my doorway, looking old and paunchy in his cardigan sweater—more like an old fart at the Elks Club than some fairy running around in the woods. "I'm suspended," he says.

In homeroom there are eyes on me. I keep my head down. I write my name, over and over, in a spiral notebook. When Miss Moynihan calls my name there are snickers from the back of the room, but she stares them down. So she knows too, I think. We watch a video about nuclear weapons.

In the hall people make faces and whisper to each other, but they stay away, which is the best I can expect. It's not like I've got an army of friends who would rush to defend me. Drew comes up and fake punches me in the stomach—I guess to let me know that we're still manly men and to let everyone else know that he, at least, is on my side. He is five-foot-three and plays snare drum in the marching band. "So, Meester Elwood," he says. "You learn the Jetsons Theme?"

"The what?"

He pushes his glasses up the bridge of his nose. "Fuck you. The cartoon medley."

I make a face.

"For today? Rehearsal? The Turkey Day game?" He waves his hand back and forth in front of my face. "Hello? Hello?"

I explain that I am dropping band. Playing clarinet is just one of several things I will not do in public for a long, long time. Others: wear pink shirts, sharpen pencils, eat bananas. Beer in long-neck bottles. Anything to do with flowers.

On the door of my locker, in indelible black magic marker, is a drawing of a man, naked, kneeling down, with another man kneeling behind him, a giant third leg standing up from his abdomen. "Gee, Dad," the cartoon voice balloon says, "why can't we just go camping, like other families?"

The *Gazette* runs a front-page story about the arraignment. There is a priest, a banker, a man who runs a Sunoco station. Then there's my father, the menace of the J. G. Whittier Middle School.

A group of parents is calling for an investigation. "We want to know, has he ever chaperoned dances? Has he supervised gym?" a man named Ralph Leighton says.

A New Hampshire state trooper describes "the activities observed at the location." He uses words like "sodomy" and "fondling." During the arrest, he says, officers wore thick rubber gloves to keep from getting AIDS. Suddenly I think of our plates, our glasses, our toilet seat: but no, I think, that's ridiculous.

A Derry selectman says he doesn't care what these guys do as long as they do it in someone else's town. "I don't hate queers," he says.

After dinner, no kidding—Dad is cleaning his shotgun. He laughs when he sees the look on my face.

"For Christ's sake, Bob." He's wearing his most Dad outfit: corduroys from L. L. Bean, a polo shirt, and a golf sweater. "I thought we'd go down to Plum Island on Saturday. Ducks are open."

We really do hunt, he and I. Deer, ducks. But Jesus, I'm thinking—what's next? A pickup truck? Drinking contests? Washing whites with colors?

Dad is sunk so deep into his recliner that he and the chair look like all one piece, as if it grew out of his back. The remarkable thing is how much like a Dad he is. He is a little too fat in the belly and ass, and his brown hair is thin on top and shot with gray on the sides. He even wears brown tortoise-shell half-glasses when he reads the newspaper.

I snap on the television and pretend to watch, but when he's not looking I study his face, looking for clues. For three days I've wondered how he managed to fool us all for so long. Wasn't there anything different about him? Yes, I realize now, there is a certain softness in his cheeks, a slackness at the edges of his mouth, which I hadn't noticed before.

"What?" he says, looking up from oiling the barrel.

"Nothing. Is that the Remington?"

He scowls. I turn back to the television and pretend to watch the commercial.

The phone rings. I jump up. "I'll unplug it."

"No," he says. He groans getting out of his chair. "Hello?" he says. Then, in a voice I've never heard: "Hi! Yes, I was hoping! I called this afternoon. Right. Oh, wait a minute." He hands me the phone. "Hang this up when I get upstairs?" Before I hang up I hear him say, "So, Mark."

In the night the phone rings. I reach, wondering how long it's been ringing.

A voice says, "You know how fags—"

I hang up. My breath rises in short, quick bursts. I think about school tomorrow. The phone rings again, and I unplug the cord, forgetting the other phones: the ringing continues in the kitchen, in the family room, in my father's room. My father says hello.

Then, groggy, he says, "Pardon me?"

I turn my face into my pillow. In the morning he pours me coffee and apologizes for the calls. "We'll get an answering machine," he says.

Mom says the Driscolls have room for me. I tell her I'm fine. "We're going hunting," I tell her. She rolls her eyes.

It's Wednesday. We're having dinner at Beshara's, a Lebanese place on South Union Street.

"Anyway, you can't all stay with the Driscolls," I say. "I mean, forever."

She says she is fully aware of what she can and can't do. She reminds me that she is my mother. I tell her I'm fully aware of that. I tell her that Dad is still Dad; that in most ways, nothing has changed. She uses words like "denial" and "trauma." She talks about lawyers and restraining orders. She pushes a cube of lamb back and forth on her plate.

"Are you going to eat that?" I say.

"Here." She slides her plate toward me.

I tell her my theory, which is that Dad has a brain tumor. Yesterday Drew told me about an uncle of his who one day at breakfast told his wife he was leaving her and the children to become a painter. And then did.

"That was Gauguin," she says.

"What?"

"Never mind."

"Anyway, something like a year later the guy had a seizure, and when they took him to the hospital they found out he had a tumor on his brain, the size of a grapefruit."

She lights a cigarette. "Why is it that tumors are always the size of a grapefruit? They're never the size of an orange. Or a cantaloupe."

This has been harder on her than I'd realized. I push on,

though, explaining to her how Drew's uncle woke after surgery and didn't even know he'd left his family—the whole thing had been a mistake.

"And they all lived happily ever after," she says.

"Not really."

She raises an eyebrow. I shake my head.

"It doesn't matter. What *does* matter is that we get Dad in for a brain scan—fast."

Finally, I make her laugh.

Our house leaks cold air through every joint, and the frame shudders and groans in the November wind. This house has been in the Abbott family since Ralph Waldo Emerson lived in our town. Emerson, in fact, ate dinner here, with my great-great-great uncle, Walter Henry Abbott.

I can't sleep. I lie still as a stone beneath two blankets and wonder whether my father fantasizes about me.

He must think about men. Young men: he must like the way we look. Does he think about me? Does he look at me? Has he ever? I cast back, but I can't remember any incidents. He sees me in the morning, though, scampering cold in a towel from the bathroom to my bedroom. I think about him eyeing me, wanting to take me in his mouth.

For a moment I wish him dead: I wonder what it would be like if he were gone. It is as if I have discovered that the man in the other room is not who he says he is; that he has been in a witness protection program and his real name is not Henry Abbott, but something else altogether, something sinister and Italian; that he is not my father at all.

I wonder if I will inherit this. I had a dream, once. But just once. And there was Art Brancato, a senior when I was a freshman: hairy-chested in the locker room, lounging naked, unafraid, a full-grown man at seventeen; I studied the way he squinted when he laughed, and for a while I tried to walk the way he did, rolling my shoulders. But no. That's not the same. In the morning there is frost on the lawn and someone has spray-painted "Honk If You Love Men" on both sides of the Cutlass. The front of the house is spattered with eggs—it looks as if something big has sneezed on us.

Thanksgiving is a week away. Drew says I can come to his family's house, but I have to turn him down. Dad says he's going to cook dinner. He's counting on me. Secretly I'm hoping that someone will invite us—Aunt Marian, maybe—but I realize that's unlikely. We are pariahs, the unclean. So we will end up, the two of us, leaning over our little turkey and thanking God— for what? For not being run over by a train? For not being hit by lightning? "Well," I imagine Dad saying in his phony classroom voice, "we've still got two good arms and two good legs. That's more than some can say."

He calls the Driscolls to see if Mom and the kids will come home for the holiday. He has not spoken to her since she left. His hand shakes so much that he misses the number and has to hang up and dial again.

"Bill? Henry. Thanks," he says when Mr. Driscoll answers. "That means a lot right now. Right. I know. It's tough on all of us. I'm calling for Kate, actually. Oh. Well, I mean, you could tell her, all I want to do is talk. I mean, what harm—OK. All right. Maybe later, then."

But later she won't take his call, either.

He goes upstairs. I hear him on the phone with Mark. I imagine he's inviting him for Thanksgiving. Before our Norman Rockwell holiday scene can take form in my mind, I hear a sound like coughing from behind his door.

"For Christ's sake," he says. "For Christ's sake. All right then. I won't. I said I won't. Bye."

I dread gym but I don't ask to be excused. Afterward, in the locker room, I can't help it: I glance at their bodies. Not between their legs, but at the legs themselves. The long muscles of the thighs. The arms, the shoulders, the chests. The curved, wing-shaped backs.

I want to know if this excites me. I have always insisted that it doesn't, but I've never actually checked.

I look at their shapes, pink in the steam of the shower room. There is something, maybe. My looks are too furtive to tell. If I stared I might feel more. Or I might feel less.

It's Thursday afternoon. Walking home I hear the band practicing in the field behind the auditorium, and I hate my father for bringing me to this.

At home, Aunt Marian, Dad's sister, is sitting on the couch. She has brought a coffee cake; she makes them for funerals. She fidgets with the cellophane wrapping. Dad's family is pure Yankee, as tight with their feelings as they are with their money. They're not equipped for this.

"Well," she says.

He plants himself into his recliner. "So, yes," he says. "Nice of you."

Kindness lasts as long as a cup of tea. She avoids all references to Thanksgiving and instead chatters on about family gossip: which cousin got which piece of furniture from Grandmother Wilkinson's house in Gloucester, why Cousin Richard needed electroshock therapy. Then, her support shown, her duty endured, she rises to leave.

At the door she says, "Has Mom called?"

"Maybe I should call her."

"Poor dear Henry." She kisses his cheek. She turns to me and I get the same kiss. "Take care, Robert."

Twice that afternoon he starts to call, then hangs up. He putters. He fixes the leak in the roof in the back porch. He cleans leaves from the rain gutters.

Mom is taking Jenny and Nelson to spend Thanksgiving in Ohio with her sister. They might not come back, she says.

She and Dad are in the kitchen, Friday afternoon. I'm in the family room, wondering what we'll call this room now. Den, maybe.

Dad says she's using her children as bargaining chips.

"There's no bargaining going on here," she says. She tells him he should get a lawyer.

He sits at the kitchen table. He looks like a guy in a Vietnam movie, mumbling about all his dead friends, too shell-shocked to think straight.

She takes out a piece of paper and begins running down a list of what they own and what their debts are. Suddenly he interrupts her, slams his hand on the table, and says, "Look, you can't goddamn *do* this. You can't."

More and more he is angry. I take this as a good sign. At least he's acting like a man. In the scenario I dread, he slides the other way: he gets a fancy haircut, shrieks at jokes, flips his hands as he speaks.

Mom doesn't flinch. She folds the paper, puts it in her purse, and snaps it shut. "Good-bye, then," she says.

I walk her to the car. We sit in the driveway. She lights a new cigarette from the old one. Her hands tremble. She says, "I really don't think you should be staying here."

"Look," I say, "I'm not going to sleep on some couch in some basement."

"Does the other guy—" She drags, then exhales. "Does he come over?"

"I think they broke up."

"Broke up." She shakes her head. "Jesus Christ." She laughs. She seems fragile, as if she's grown old too fast, like the plants in those sped-up film clips. I can't look at her. "Bob," she says, "I want you to come with us to Ohio."

Don't do this, I'm thinking. Don't make me choose. In seven months I will finish school and then I will leave them all; but for now I want things to stay the same.

"I can get a court order," she says. "You're a minor."

Across the street, Mr. Gauthier is on his lawn, raking leaves and watching us. I wave at him. He looks away.

"Bob, please," she says.

"Reveille," Dad says. It's Saturday morning, still dark out. "Rise and shine."

We stop at Big Bear for coffee and cinnamon rolls. On the way to Plum Island I fall back to sleep, and when I wake up we are backing down the boat ramp. We have rented a Nissan Sentra while the Cutlass is being painted.

I winch out the boat, a twelve-foot Sears aluminum rowboat with a three-horse Evinrude motor, then drag it ashore with the bow line while Dad parks.

We sputter down the channel into the thick of the salt marsh, then sit and wait. The dawn sky is sick gray. I worry that it might rain. Dad loads five shells into the chamber of his gas-action Remington and hands me two for my over-and-under, the gun he used as a boy. We sit facing each other, barrels across our laps. We wait. We wait some more.

"Open those sardines," he says.

This is our hunting breakfast, a habit he got from his father. It's a tradition I don't plan to carry on.

The tin cover sticks at first. I take off my gloves to get a better grip, and when I pull harder the lid suddenly tears off in my hand

12

and runs a long, curved slice across the meat of my thumb. "Fuck," I say, because we swear when we hunt. "Motherfucker," I say, as a line of blood fills the cut.

Dad reaches across and takes my hand. "Let's have a look," he says, but his touch is like a spark, and I pull away.

He stops. His eyes are wide open. He starts to say something, then doesn't. I look out over the marsh. There is nothing but water and sky, all gray. I imagine us from above, in black and white, so small on the water. I place the tin of sardines on the bench seat between us. I squeeze my thumb in the palm of my other hand. A drop of blood hits the bottom of the boat with a splat. Another falls; then another.

He reaches back to the first-aid box and takes out a Band-Aid. "Here," he says. I hold out my thumb, and he wraps the cut.

We sit. He doesn't say anything. He stares at me. I put my gloves back on. The wake from a boat crossing the marsh rocks us clumsily. He's still staring.

"I'm sorry," I say finally. "I just can't understand."

He fidgets with his wool cap. "I know."

"Maybe someday. I don't know."

"But you still love your old man, don't you?"

I kick my boots together. "Don't ask me things like that."

I look up. His eyes are reaching. I'm thinking that whatever happens, I don't want to see him cry.

"I need to know that," he says. "It's important."

He tries to take my hand again, but again I pull away.

"Stop it," I say. I sit back away from him. "Just don't."

He droops. I consider starting the engine and heading out of the marsh. But as awful as this moment is, I am unable to let it go. I feel on the edge of a discovery, as if some truth is about to reveal itself.

It doesn't. We sit and wait without talking. The water is calm, and now that the sun has come up, it's almost warm. We eat the sardines on crackers.

Suddenly shots are booming out over the water all around us—I realize now we're not alone here—and looking up I see the first line of ducks arcing down into the marsh. I point over his shoulder and he wheels and drops to one knee but already we're too late, they're past us and banking off, but he fires and fires anyway, long after the others have stopped. With each shot the recoil kicks his right shoulder back, as if it might spin him around. The spent shells leap from his chamber and hit the bottom of the boat still smoking, and he fires, fires, and fires into the empty sky.

He collapses into the curve of the bow. He turns his face away. I crawl over and kneel by him. "Dad," I say, "they're gone." He takes my hand, and this time I let him keep it.

Our new Code-A-Phone is chirping, and the message light blinks in time with it. Dad drops his hunting gear in the corner and, still in his plaid wool coat and right in front of me, he rushes to the machine like a schoolgirl. There is a man's voice, and I'm thinking, I really don't want to hear this.

But it's a man named Duncan Gardner, a lawyer. He represents Mom. "From now on, if you want to talk, I'd like you to talk to me," he says.

There are no other messages. Dad stands there, realizing, I guess, how foolish he looks. He takes a bottle to bed.

Later, past midnight, I lie awake in bed. Outside, the first snow of the season is falling against the night sky, tumbling through the tree branches and ticking against my window, and it's as if all the trouble in the world is coming down on us. Our old house creaks. I watch the snow toss and mingle in the air.

Dad is stirring in his room. Then his door opens and he pads down the stairs, through the hall and across the kitchen. I hold myself still, expecting—and I admit, half-hoping—to hear the crack of a muffled report from the garage. At least then we all could get over this. Instead there is the hum of the refrigerator, the clink of a bottle, a kitchen chair scraping on the linoleum floor. I cannot imagine why, but my poor father has decided to trudge on, and I know there are worse times ahead.

I think of him down there alone in the dark. I think of my mother, sleeping on a couch in someone's house. I think of Drew's uncle with the brain tumor, whose wife was so glad to have him back from the hospital that she decorated the house with balloons and streamers and threw a party for him. What they couldn't know, as they passed around the pieces of cake and danced to Ray Charles records, was that in three months his liver and lungs would be rotten with cancer, and that a month after that he'd be dead, leaving his friends to feel small and stupid—scared of the future, and stunned by the secrets life buries in us.

Violet

ON SATURDAY Anna arrived with the cat. Sophie had seen photographs of Anna—there was the one Gordon kept hidden in his sock drawer, its edges thumbed and creased like an old piece of leather—but in real life she was more, well, *imposing*.

She pulled the curtain aside and watched through the bay window as Anna unloaded the cat's gear from her car. Anna, Gordon's wife, was a writer for a magazine in Boston. She also had written a children's book which she had been unable to publish. She was short and thin, with small breasts and thick dark hair that fell past her shoulders. She walked with her arms hanging loose at her sides, with a threatening, hip-rolling gait. She wore a pair of jeans with holes in the knees and a man's plain white T-shirt with no bra underneath.

Anna had left Gordon for another man. Now she was leaving the new man, too, and she said she needed Gordon to keep Violet until she found a new apartment. She was staying with a friend in the Back Bay, but the friend was allergic to cats. Yesterday she'd called and left a message on the machine, calling herself Anna Phelan—which was Gordon's last name; they were still married, officially—and saying, "We need to talk. It's about Violet." Sophie had played the message over and over, listening to Anna's deep, bossy voice and wondering who on earth Violet could be. Later, when Gordon came home and explained about the cat, she told him he was a fool to even talk to Anna, let alone to do her favors. But now there he was, a grown man—a dentist, in fact—standing in the driveway with a litter box in one hand and a bag of cat toys in the other.

They came up the steps. Anna put down a bag of cat food and wiped her hand on her jeans. "Well, you must be Sophie." She laughed. "Gordie's told me a lot about you."

"And I've heard a lot about you," Sophie said.

They needed several trips to bring in all the gear: a litter box and plastic sieve-scoop, a travel cage, a toy dolphin that squeaked, a cloth ball with little tin bells sewn into the cover, medicine, dry food, wet food, bowls, dishes, flea collars. "This is a nightmare," Sophie said as the pile of cat equipment grew in the kitchen.

Gordon took her hand. "It's just for a little while."

At last Anna came inside with the cat. Violet was small, with black-and-white spotted fur. She clung by her claws to Anna's T-shirt. "She gets nervous in a new place," Anna said. She rubbed her nose on the cat's face. "Don't you, little pumpkin?"

The cat licked Anna's cheek. Sophie gasped; she could not imagine letting that awful little tongue ever touch her.

Gordon took the cat and spoke in the same baby-talk voice: "You like it here, Violet? Sure, sure you do. You want to meet Sophie?"

Sophie took a step back. "That's OK."

Anna said, "You're not afraid of cats, are you?"

"I'm not afraid. I just don't like them."

Gordon held the cat out toward her. It hung slack over his hand, with its paws dangling. "Here, just try holding her. Let her get used to you."

"Thanks anyway."

He moved closer.

"Gordon," she said.

He wiggled the cat's paw, to make it look as if it were waving at her. "It's just little Violet," he said.

"Gordon, no. For Christ's sake."

Anna laughed. "OK. Here, Gordie, give her back to me." She cradled the cat in her arm and stroked its head with her index finger. "There, baby. Oh, listen—can you hear her purring?"

From the cat came a sound like a plastic rattle. It made Sophie's skin crawl to imagine how this animal could produce such a sound. Already the kitchen bore the faint pungent odor of cat.

On her way out Anna stopped in the living room and commented on the print above the couch, which was a close-up painting of a flower with swollen red stamens. "I have this theory about people who like O'Keeffe," she said.

"You should write an article about it," Sophie said. "Or a book, maybe."

She picked up the *Gazette*, sat down, and pretended to read. Gordon walked Anna out to her car and watched her drive away. He stood in the driveway, waving like a fool.

Sophie and Gordon had been seeing each other for less than six months when they took the house on Packard Street. Their first fight had come on moving day. This happened when he started to carry his queen-sized bed, the bed he had shared with Anna, through the front door.

"Just turn right around right now," she said, "before we have to call a priest and have the house exorcised."

"For God's sake," he said. "What is this? You're superstitious or something?"

They went back and forth. He pushed; she pushed back. She tried to be nice. But finally she moved from conciliation to demand. "We're using my bed, and that's that," she said.

He reminded her that her bed was a double. He stood in the doorway, with the frame of his bed teetering on his shoulder. "Two people can't sleep in a double," he said.

She smiled and reminded him that a double, after all, was made for two people. "Hence the name," she said.

He put down the frame and wiped his forehead with a handkerchief. Gordon was stubborn—bull-headed, even; she supposed you'd have to be to get through dental school—and for a while it appeared the argument would go on all night and they'd end up sleeping on the lawn; so finally she offered to go out and buy a new bed. "Queen size," she said. "All right?"

He shrugged.

She kissed his cheek. "Now just take that thing out to the garage and leave it there. Better yet, put it out with the trash. Or burn it."

So she had won that battle. But there would be others. The kitchen set, the armoire, the living-room couch—all of them were things Gordon had dragged with him out of his marriage. They were ugly, horrible pieces: faux colonial monstrosities from Ethan Allen; gruesomely ornate imitation Victorian chairs; Monet prints you'd expect to see in a high school girl's room. Monet, for Christ's sake! Gordon and Anna had bought them when they were first married, before they had money. "Or taste," Sophie said.

Now, though, they had been living together for four months and she had managed to get rid of Gordon's old junk and redecorate the house in a kind of modified southwestern style. The main piece was an oak couch with an orange-to-blue flame-stitch pattern. She had hung O'Keeffe prints and put out a bleached cow skull and Indian pottery—"Native American," the Newbury Street salesman had sniffed.

She was only twenty-four, eight years younger than Gordon, but on those afternoons when she curled up on the couch with a cup of Red Zinger tea and admired the job she'd done on the house, the worries she'd had about being too young or too naive seemed to fly away, and she believed she knew as much about life as anyone. She subscribed to the Sunday *Times*, she made thirty-five thousand a year doing public relations for Ionic Software Corp., and until Violet became her house guest she secretly believed that her life was better than she deserved.

They put the cat's litter box and toys in the kitchen, in the corner by the back door. Gordon ran off to play golf. He retreated from confrontation. If they couldn't agree on something, he would change the subject or just stop talking altogether. Sometimes he would get up and go to another room. He was perfect as a dentist: she imagined him in his office, dealing all day with people whose mouths were propped open and who could not talk back to him.

Violet was playing in the kitchen. The bells of her toy ball tinkled as she batted it across the floor. Then the cat started scratching in her litter box and Sophie began to feel queasy. She lay on the couch and tried to read, but she was distracted and couldn't make her way into the book. Every so often she'd stop and realize she couldn't remember the last three pages, and she'd have to back up and read them over.

Then Violet became quiet, and Sophie couldn't read at all. She lay still and listened for the cat. She was afraid to fall asleep, for fear that it would spring on her. At last she got up and went to the kitchen, where she found Violet curled up on the kitchen counter by the canisters of flour and sugar, sleeping.

"Shoo," she said. "Violet. You can't sleep near the food. Shoo."

Violet opened her droopy eyelids, looked at Sophie, then shut her eyes and went back to sleep.

Sophie got a broom and brushed the tip across the counter. "Shoo." She shook the broom. "Violet. Hey." At last she poked the cat with the broom. It jumped up with a start. Sophie dropped the broom. "OK. Get down. Get away from the food."

Violet arched her back, then stretched out her front paws, yawned, and lay back down.

Sophie was still standing there, broom in hand, wondering what to do, when Gordon clattered in carrying his golf bag and cleated shoes. His face and arms were sunburned.

"Honey," she said, "the cat's up near the food. I can't get it down."

He set his golf bag in the corner and suggested she call the fire department.

"I don't want it near the food," she said. She handed him the broom. "Here, get it down."

He lifted the cat from the counter and set it on the floor. Violet ran off down the hall, then rushed back to the kitchen and sprang onto a chair. Gordon picked her up and held her against his chest.

"Can't we keep it someplace?" Sophie said. "Like in the spare bedroom?"

The cat peered over Gordon's arm and squinted its eyes. "Look—it made a face at me," she said.

"Sophie, for God's sake, it's a she, not an it, and maybe if you petted her a little she'd get to know you."

"I don't want to get to know it," Sophie said.

That night Gordon made Thai soup. Sophie found a hair in her bowl and couldn't eat, even though Gordon insisted the hair was not from the cat.

This was Saturday night, so when they went to bed Gordon didn't want to sleep right away. Since they'd moved in together, his sex drive had fallen into a pattern: Saturday night; Sunday afternoon; Wednesday or Thursday night. Maybe a random morning.

He began to kiss her body. His whiskers chafed her skin. On weekends he didn't shave; that fall he'd bought a Range Rover, and now he thought of himself as an outdoorsman. But the scrub on his face looked ridiculous, and when they went out on weekends, to the supermarket or the video store, Sophie was embarrassed for him.

"Gordon, stop," she said.

He poked his head up from under the sheet.

"Your whiskers," she said. She rubbed his cheek. "They're scratching me."

"They tickle, remember?" He moved his hand between her legs. "Remember?"

She pulled his hand away. "They scratch," she said.

"Sophie." He kissed her belly.

She grabbed his hair. "Gordon, please. Go shave."

He groaned, then shuffled out to the bathroom. When he returned he wasn't interested. They lay on their backs, staring up at the dark. Outside, the bug light sizzled, then stopped, and the yard was silent.

Sophie tried, but she could not make Violet like her. Every time she looked at the cat she thought of Anna, with her T-shirt and no bra and her strange, gray eyes. Sometimes it was as if Anna, and not Violet, was the one curled up in the sunbeam, or tossing a stuffed mouse around the floor.

She was convinced that Violet resented her for having taken Anna's place. Pets could sense this kind of thing. When she went to the spare bedroom to play with Violet—she'd promised Gordon that she would make an effort—the cat would ignore her. One time she snapped at Sophie's finger; Sophie took the toy dolphin, Violet's favorite toy, and put it up on the dresser, out of reach.

The worst thing was that the cat gave Anna an excuse to call Gordon. He complained about how this annoyed him, but it was clear that some part of him enjoyed the calls. Sophie didn't know what to say. There was no evidence; she felt like one of those harping wives in old movies. "I don't like this," was the best she could do.

Gordon smiled and patted her hand. He acted the way her father did when she got upset at home. He said she was ridiculous to worry. But then one night he came out from talking to Anna on the phone and said he had agreed to let her come visit the cat.

"In my house?"

"Relax," he said. "It's only for a while."

So Anna began to visit, usually on Saturday afternoons. Sophie would arrange to be out at those times; she'd do errands or shop for clothes at the mall. This was an unusual arrangement, certainly, but then her life was not the usual life. On those Saturdays, as she sat in Friendly's drinking coffee and waiting for the clock to strike five, she calmed herself by remembering that all this was temporary, and in the end everything would work out.

But as time went on the spare bedroom began to reek of cat odor, and Sophie became more and more certain that something was going on between Gordon and Anna. They talked every night on the phone; it couldn't be just about the cat. He'd shut himself up in the spare bedroom and would be in there for almost an hour sometimes, laughing.

One night when he hadn't come home by six o'clock she called his office and got the answering service. They said he'd left at five.

When he got home it was past seven. He said he'd had a last-minute patient. "This Korean guy. Honey, his breath smelled like he'd been eating dog meat or something."

"The service said you left at five," she said.

"Imbeciles." He picked up a pencil, then put it down. "I've got to get a new service."

"So you were there."

"Of course I was." He put his arms around her. "This Korean guy, Sophie, I swear, you should've seen him. An abscess like you wouldn't believe."

His breath smelled of alcohol. "Gordon," she said.

"I wanted to pour Lysol down his throat. 'Kimchi,' he says, and gives me this big smile."

He kissed her. Her tongue came away with the taste of scotch, and other things she didn't want to imagine.

A few nights later Gordon called to say he was having dinner with Anna. "We've got to talk out some terms," he said.

"Terms," Sophie said.

"That's right. For the divorce."

"Is your lawyer going, too?"

"Honey," he said. "Come on. Give me a break."

She made a salad, but she couldn't eat. The smell from the cat's room had fouled the house. Finally she went to that room and emptied the litter box, a chore Gordon had promised she'd never have to perform.

The whole time, as she sifted through the litter with the sieve-scoop and tossed the smelly pebbles into the trash, she imagined Gordon and Anna in a booth at Beshara's eating hummus and grape leaves and lamb on the stick, while she was here, stooping over a litter box. Fine, she thought. Let him spend some time with her, and he'll remember why they broke up in the first place. The thing to do was to stay calm and give him time to work things out. If she got angry it would just drive him away. This was exactly what Anna wanted, of course—but she wasn't going to give her the satisfaction. As she left the room the cat tried to sneak out between her ankles, but she kicked it back into the center of the room and jumped out before it could recover. She was aware of a mild sense of pleasure, like the beginning of a sneeze, that she'd got from seeing Violet stunned like that.

Behind the door the cat was crying and scratching to get out. Sophie went to the living room, stretched out on the couch, put on a pair of headphones and tuned to the jazz station. She closed her eyes and tried not to think about the damage Violet was doing to the woodwork.

When she woke it was dark. She took off the headphones and was startled to hear Anna's laughter coming from down the hallway. She went to the kitchen.

There was a bottle of wine on the table, almost empty.

"Hey, it's Sophie," Gordon said. He slid a chair out for her. "Here, sit down."

She slid the chair back under the table. "Why didn't you wake me up?"

Anna stood up. "Well, I'd better be going."

"Already?" Gordon held up the wine bottle. "Look, there's still some left."

Sophie stayed in the kitchen while Gordon walked Anna out to the front door. She heard them mumbling, then chuckling about something.

"Call me," Gordon said.

She went to bed and lay in the dark with her eyes open. She remembered the weekend when they'd driven to Boothbay Harbor and stayed in a bed-and-breakfast near the water, and how they had both pretended to like shopping for antiques because they thought the other one did. She remembered the night when Gordon took her to her first Red Sox game and she ate sausage-and-onion sandwiches and they worried that they might run into Anna because she lived in the Back Bay, near Fenway Park. But they didn't see Anna; in those days Gordon went out of his way to keep her as far from their lives as possible. At night, in those days, Sophie would return to her own little studio apartment; sometimes it was nice to just kiss Gordon goodnight and go inside and sleep alone.

If she had that apartment now, she thought, she could go curl up on her couch and watch a movie. She'd turn off the phone and let Gordon's calls go through to the machine and not listen to the tape until the next morning, when she felt better. She rolled over onto her side.

He opened the door. "Sophie? What are you doing?"

She didn't answer.

"Sophie, it's nine thirty. What's the matter?"

She looked over her shoulder. "Are you serious?"

He sat down on the bed beside her. The mattress sagged under his weight. "Of course I'm serious," he said.

She took a deep breath. She did not want to get angry. She said, in a voice as calm as if she were asking for a glass of water, that she wanted to know what was going on between him and Anna.

"Are you kidding?" he said. "The woman walked out on me, for Christ's sake." He laid his arm across her belly. "Which is probably the best thing that ever happened to me, since I got to meet you."

He kissed her cheek. She smiled. He ran his hand up her belly, then circled her breast. She shivered.

He kissed her neck, then her breast. She felt warmth rising inside her. She ran her fingers through his hair, then began to unbutton his shirt.

"Honey," she said, "I want you to do me a favor."

"Name it."

"I want to get rid of the cat."

He ran a hand down over her belly, then lower. "We're trying," he said.

She pushed his face away. "For Christ's sake, Gordon, that's exactly what I mean," she said.

He sat up as if he'd been slapped. "*Now* what's the matter?"

"It's this *we* thing. I don't like you and Anna being a *we*. Understand? I don't like you having dinner with her. And I don't like her being in my house."

"We're friends, honey. You're going to have to accept that."

"I don't have to accept anything. Not in my house."

"Sophie," he said, "it's *our* house. Not yours."

She lay back and put her hands behind her head. "Well, if that's the way you feel," she said.

"Then what?" His face had gone red. "If that's the way I feel, then what?"

But now she didn't want to fight. She stared out the window and wondered how she had come to be here, living in New England with this dentist. At last he got up from the bed. "Please close the door," she said.

Sophie had grown up in Michigan, in a town near Saginaw, and she could not remember her parents ever having a fight. They were second-generation German, and they treated each other, if not with affection, at least with respect. In those little towns there was a certain way of acting when you were married. You didn't have your old boyfriends and old girlfriends, or ex-husbands and ex-wives, hanging around the house all the time. If you had someone from the past, they were just that—the past. You didn't keep the past alive and hovering all around you.

Here in Massachusetts people were crazy. They hated everyone with dark skin or a different accent, they drove like idiots, they were rude in line at the supermarket, and the Lawton Falls accent—*youse* and *dem* and *pahk ovah theah*—was as coarse and low class as anything she'd ever heard.

She hated it here. The morning after the fight she went to work but couldn't concentrate. She was too upset to work. She had press calls to make, trying to place stories about a new groupware product, but she couldn't concentrate. She kept forgetting what it was she wanted to say. Once she dialed a number and then forgot, when the person answered, which reporter she had called.

She stared at the photograph of her and Gordon that she kept on the shelf above her desk. The photograph showed Gordon with his arm around her. They were wearing bathing suits, standing on the beach at Cozumel under a thatched umbrella, smiling. How did you go from that to this, she wondered—for the only thing she could remember of that trip now was the terrible sunburn she'd gotten.

Finally it was too much. She gave up. She told her boss she felt sick, and she left at noon.

What she found at home almost knocked her down. Violet had escaped from her room and gone on a rampage in the living room. The rubber plant lay in ribbons at the base of its pot. The Sunday paper was torn to pieces and scattered all over the floor. And the new couch—the cat had clawed the cushions until the fabric was frayed and shredded and loose threads dangled everywhere. And there, in the middle of a cushion, sat Violet, bending over and licking herself. She sat up and tilted her head to the side.

Sophie didn't scream. She didn't yell or chase the cat around the house. She put down her briefcase, took a deep breath, scooped up the cat, removed its collar, and drove to the SPCA in Newburyport, a town several miles down the river. She explained that she and her husband had found this stray and had been feeding it.

"Well, she seems like such a friendly little thing," the woman at the counter said.

"Oh, she's wonderful. But we can't have pets."

The woman put Violet in a cage by the side of the room. She handed Sophie a form. Sophie filled in a false name and address. The cat tilted her head to the side and gazed at her, wide eyed, through the wire cage.

She completed the form and passed the clipboard back. She nodded toward Violet. "What do you, ah, do with them?"

The woman hitched up her belt. "Well, we try to find them homes. But if we can't, well, after three days we put them down."

"Oh." Sophie opened her purse, then snapped it shut. "Well, thank you."

Driving home she told herself it was only a cat, after all. The bottom line was that she was doing the right thing. The cat had been forced on her. She had been too kind already. If anyone was to blame, it was Anna, who should have known better than to try to weasel her way back into Gordon's life. In Saginaw they called this "worming," and girls who did it had their clothes stolen from their lockers while they were in the shower. One time her best friend, Greta Hoehn, had been carried out and thrown into a snowbank, naked, just as the hockey team was getting out of practice.

"I can't believe you're this upset," she said.

Gordon had just returned. He had been gone for hours, driving around the neighborhood looking for Violet.

"You can't believe? This is my cat, Sophie—my pet. I've had it for four years."

I thought it was Anna's cat."

"Well, it was both of ours."

"But it's just a cat."

"I've got to call Anna. Jesus Christ. I'll call her from Violet's room."

He took the phone to the spare bedroom. Sophie went to the bedroom, got into bed, and tried to read a magazine. Through the wall she heard him pleading. Then she heard him in the backyard, making little kissing noises and calling out Violet's name. The sound of his voice was haunting. She remembered him telling her how when Anna left him he had followed her outside and stood on the front lawn, begging her not to drive away. She got up and looked out the window and watched him in the darkened yard, searching the bushes with a flashlight and calling to Violet.

Finally he shuffled inside. "Well, I left a dish of food out for her."

He undressed and crawled into bed. He picked up the remote and switched on the television.

"Don't," she said. She switched the television off, then ran her hand over his chest. "Come here."

"For what?"

"You know." She kissed his neck. "Relax."

"Sophie, come on. How could I, with all this going on? Jesus." He switched on the television again and scanned through the channels.

The next night Gordon called the SPCA in Lawton Falls. He knocked on every door in the neighborhood, asking if they'd seen his cat. He drove through all the neighborhoods, stopping to tape up flyers that offered a reward. Finally, again, he stood out in the backyard with his flashlight, calling to Violet. Sophie opened the window and whispered to him that he should think of the neighbors.

"I don't care what they think."

"What about me, then?"

"Well." He clicked the flashlight off, then on. "I don't know."

He started calling again. She shut the window. He kept calling for half an hour more.

In the morning Anna called to say she would come up that evening to help hunt for the cat. Sophie drove off in a huff, only to see Gordon's posters taped to every telephone pole she passed. This was too much. She couldn't imagine another night of listening to him pining away in the backyard. During her lunch break she drove to the SPCA in Newburyport and told the woman—there was a different woman this time—that she wanted Violet. The woman went out back, but returned without the cat.

"She's gone," the woman said.

"What—someone took her? Where is she?"

"She must've been in the bunch they did this morning," the woman said.

"Did? What do you mean, *did?*"

"I'm sorry."

"You mean—"

The woman nodded. Sophie felt blood pounding in her ears. "The other woman told me we had three days."

"This is the third day." She took Sophie's hand. "I really am sorry."

"No, no. I understand." She made her way out to her car, then sat behind the wheel for several minutes, trying to collect herself.

She remembered how Violet had liked to roll her toy ball across the kitchen floor, then bat it up against the cabinets. She hadn't been a bad cat, really. She'd just got into the middle of something.

Sophie imagined going home that night and listening to Gordon in the backyard again. And Anna—now Anna would be there, too. She thought of all the lies she'd heard from them already, and all the ones she'd have to hear in the future. And now she was lying, too. She was becoming as crazy as they were. She remembered Greta Hoehn, sitting Indian-style on her bed, saying love was a form of insanity—but Sophie didn't believe it then, and she didn't believe it now.

She started the car and sat for a moment listening to the muffled hum of the engine. Then she pulled out of the dirt parking lot and drove along the river to Lawton Falls, to the real estate company that managed her old apartment building. They still had her file; there were no forms to fill out. She wrote a check for the deposit and the first month's rent.

"Would you like to see the unit?" the man asked.

She shook her head. She knew what it would look like. She knew exactly how everything would be.

The Miracle

THERE WAS NOT MUCH case to be made for Holy Trinity. The church was on Common Street, in Little Italy, and in the years since the Italians had moved to the suburbs the parish had dwindled: Masses were nearly empty, save for a handful of widows and a band of charismatic Catholics called "Vita Dei" who held healing ceremonies in the church courtyard during the summer. The church was ninty-six years old; it was an immigrant church, built of granite and cement, plain poor gray, with a modest spire topped by a cross and a steep roof of dark slate shingles that leaked during the spring rains. The school out back had been closed for years. The nuns were gone, and their convent was empty. And now the whole place would be torn down.

"I don't believe it," Father Catalano said.

"I still don't quite either," Monsignor D'Agostino said.

Only an hour before, D'Agostino had been in the cardinal's residence in Framingham getting the news: Lawton Falls needed elderly housing; the best site belonged to an Elks Club, but they wouldn't sell to a man named Cardinal *Mendosa;* and so Holy Trinity, the poorest of Lawton Falls' thirty-seven parishes, would be sacrificed.

"I suppose now they'll send me off to a home," Catalano said. He rolled over on his bed and, as he did, his undershirt rode up over his belly. "Once they decide on these things . . . I've been around long enough to know . . . I've seen it happen . . . nobody lasts very long in those places . . . well, but there's no changing minds with these people," he said.

He began to cry. D'Agostino didn't like to watch it; he looked away, out the window, into the maple trees whose branch tips had begun to swell with buds so red and raw that it seemed as if the trees themselves ached. The old curate was seventy-three years old and he had been at Holy Trinity for most of his life. He smoked a pack of cigarettes a day and drank blended whiskey from a bottle that he kept in his closet. For years D'Agostino had written sermons for him, and each morning he took the early Mass so that the old man could sleep.

"I won't last long in a place like that," he said.

"Don't talk like that," D'Agostino said.

"Have you told your mother?"

"I'll see her tonight."

James Keegan, the secretary to the cardinal, had promised to let D'Agostino's mother have first choice of the new archdiocese apartments. She was not impressed by the offer.

"I don't take gifts from *mulis*," she said when he explained the situation.

"Mom," he told her, "he's a Cuban."

She waved her hand. "He's a *muli*."

They were in her living room, in the house on Prospect Street where he'd grown up: a little Depression-era Italian home where nothing moved or changed, where even the dust seemed to hang in the air. The couch was covered with plastic, and the walls were covered with photographs: his father and mother at their wedding; his father in an army uniform; high school portraits of Carmine and Maria and Michael; Michael's ordination;

Maria's children, Carmine's children; and now the children of those children, all the chubby babies and gangly teenagers. "You always let them push you around," she said. "Carmine says it's embarrassing, the way they push you around." As a boy he had been so terrified of his mother that he had developed a stutter in her presence. She was eighty-one years old now, and in the last few years she had developed arthritis and had begun to have trouble walking; she was calcifying, turning hard.

"Carmine doesn't understand the church," he said.

"Then neither do I," she said.

He sat in the naugahyde recliner that had been his father's chair and which even now, a decade after his death, still bore his smell.

"Your father wouldn't let this happen," she said.

"Oh? What would Dad do?"

But she just laughed and looked down at her lap.

When he arrived back at the rectory the Vita Dei charismatics were standing on the front steps of the church bundled up in ski parkas, carrying picket signs and handing out leaflets to people walking by on Common Street. A light rain was falling; they stood under umbrellas. Standing in front was Enzo Russo, a fire department captain who had grown up in Little Italy and who claimed to have been cured of pancreatic cancer by a charismatic priest from Worcester. Beside him was Rita Torresi, a woman from Poplar Street who once had asked D'Agostino to sell her pre-Vatican II Mass books. He'd refused; the old Mass was outlawed. "Father," she'd said, her green eyes lolling from side to side as if they'd come unfastened, "someone has to keep the true church alive." Soon after that there was a rumor about people meeting to say the old Mass in a basement on Prospect Hill.

When he got out of his car to open the courtyard gate, they swarmed him. There were perhaps a dozen people, including three young men whom D'Agostino recognized as firefighters; in summer they sat with Enzo Russo in wooden chairs outside the neighborhood fire station on Newbury Street and said hello to him as he walked by. He did not go to their charismatic ceremonies, but he had heard enough to be convinced that they were crazy: they thrashed and flailed and spoke in tongues; the sick approached the altar and hurled themselves down, hoping Jesus would cast out their demons and cure them. They traveled by bus to New York to see a woman who claimed she had visions in which the Blessed Mother spoke to her.

"What's going on here?" D'Agostino said.

"We're having a prayer vigil," Rita Torresi said. "We're gathering our energy to drive out Satan."

"And," Enzo Russo said, "we're giving out leaflets."

He handed one to D'Agostino. On the cover was a drawing of the devil.

"This isn't the work of Satan," D'Agostino said. "It's the work of the cardinal. It's a business decision."

Rita Torresi stared at him, as if expecting to see some evidence of possession. Her eyes darted from side to side as they had before; he wondered if this was some sort of nervous condition.

"You can believe what you want to believe," she said. "We're going to be out here day and night. We'll chain ourselves to the altar if we have to."

A cheer went up from the group. D'Agostino had been about to recommend that they write letters to the cardinal; but instead he opened the gate, drove his little Ford Escort into the courtyard, and shut the gate behind him. He made sure the latch was locked.

On Wednesday a crew of engineers from a company called Advo arrived to survey the church. The Vita Dei picketers hissed and chanted and spat at them, but the engineers had a letter from the cardinal and so D'Agostino let them into the courtyard. He sat in a pew while they took Polaroid photographs and measured the width and length of the church with a wheel device that they'd brought in from the trunk of their car. The man in charge said they'd never "done" a church before; it might be tricky, he said. He took a deep breath and said, "Jeez, smell that incense, huh?"

D'Agostino excused himself and walked outside to the courtyard.

The parish buildings—the rectory, the convent, and the school—were arranged in a cluster behind the church and enclosed by a ten-foot cement wall. Within the enclosure there was a small vegetable garden, a shrine to the Blessed Mother, and a ring of maple trees that provided enough shade to keep the courtyard cool in summer. Holy Trinity was at the corner of Common and Newbury streets, among the bakeries and cafes and flower shops—and yet the courtyard was so quiet that it was easy to forget that there was a city outside.

D'Agostino's life here was quiet, and lonely, but it was peaceful. He lived from season to season, Christmas to Easter to Christmas, and while this life was boring (Carmine and Maria would go crazy) he found the boredom comforting. To have peace you had to reduce your life to only the essential things; he accepted that.

He began each day before dawn, rising to say the six-o'clock Mass. It was those moments—when he stepped into the cool air and hurried in the dark along the path to the back of the church, or when he stood in the sacristy, alone, counting the hosts, filling the glass cruets with wine and water, buttoning his cassock, pulling his vestments over his head, taking his chalice to the altar, lighting the candles—that he felt most like a priest.

Carmine said he was selfish; Maria said he was dysfunctional.

She said Michael was just afraid of having what she called a "real" life, which as far as he could tell meant such things as shopping malls and video rentals, unpleasant jobs and vacations in Disneyland. What kind of life was that? The life of the spirit, the life of the mind—he tried to explain this to them, tried to explain the bliss of giving yourself up to something more important than yourself. But they could not imagine anything more important than themselves. They had no idea; none at all.

It was Lent, the week before Palm Sunday. The Sunday after that would be Easter. Each day at six o'clock there were the same people: Rita Torresi reading from her own Mass book which she carried in her purse; Enzo Russo and a few other firefighters in their uniforms, going to Mass before starting their shift at the station; a burly, bearded man in a wheelchair who came every day; and three old widows in black shawls who sat together, eight pews back. The widows said the rosary during Mass and paid no attention to D'Agostino, other than to stand and sit and kneel at the appropriate times. Sometimes he tried to imagine what God would see if He were to look down at them; how strange our tiny group must look in that big cavernous stone church, he thought. He ran through the service quickly, skipped the hymns, gave no sermon, and was done by 6:25. Each day he secretly offered the Mass to St. Anthony, asking him to undo the cardinal's plan.

One morning Enzo Russo and Rita Torresi came to the rectory after Mass and asked if they could speak to him in private. They had been picketing outside the church every day and every night, and their following had grown. The night before, D'Agostino had peered out from his bedroom window to see fifty people milling around in front of the church, holding candles and singing "Sons of God."

He showed them in. They sat on the couch. "Father," Enzo said, "we talked to Davio."

Rita's eyes darted. "He's got a plan," she said.

"He told us to ask you first," Enzo said.

D'Agostino sighed. "I see."

Davio Giaccalone was the owner of Caffe Tripoli. He wore shiny jogging suits and gold rings and neck chains; he drove a Cadillac Fleetwood and carried a cellular phone. He and Carmine had been friends in high school. When you grew up in Little Italy you could not help knowing these types; but unlike his brother, D'Agostino did his best to avoid them.

"And what is Davio's plan?" he said.

For a moment they didn't speak. Then Enzo cleared his throat and said, "He won't say. But I'm sure it'd work."

"You know Davio," Rita said.

"Yes," he said, trying not to roll his eyes. "I know Davio."

He told them to forget it. He said he had decided to go to the Elks and make a personal plea.

"Father," Rita Torresi said, "these are men who name themselves after animals."

"Yes, I know that," D'Agostino said.

A date was set for the demolition: May 4, a Monday. The engineers came back every day with compasses and note pads and walkie-talkies on their belts, and their work took on a new urgency. They clomped through the sacristy as if it were a locker room; one of them tracked mud into the church and left his footprints all over the rug in front of the tabernacle. One man was hit by a rock as he walked through the picketers and he had to be taken to the hospital. From then on the police kept an officer stationed outside the church.

Father Catalano went around the rectory muttering to himself the phrase from the crucifixion: "Eli, Eli, lama sabach-thani?" My God, My God, why have You forsaken Me? He would sit for hours in the church watching the engineers work. One day D'Agostino found him in a pew near the back, crying softly, smelling of whiskey. "This is unbearable," he said.

As the week wore on D'Agostino became more and more panicked; his heart fluttered in his chest so desperately that he would have to sit down and catch his breath. What could he do? Every day he called Keegan and asked to speak to Cardinal Mendosa, but each time the answer was no. He called a friend who worked for the cardinal in Minneapolis, asking if he could have the cardinal there talk to Mendosa. There wasn't much they could do, his friend said.

A reporter from the *Gazette* called; they'd talked to Enzo Russo and Rita Torresi, and they were doing a story. D'Agostino gave an interview over the phone. The next day there was a story on the front page, in which Enzo Russo called the cardinal "a Cuban birdbrain" and Rita Torresi vowed that God would not stand for this kind of disrespect.

The story prompted a call from Keegan, who said the cardinal had been receiving threatening phone calls.

"What kind of people have you got up there?" he said.

"Angry," D'Agostino said. "Unhappy."

Enzo Russo called every day and left messages with Father Catalano; the old man marked each one with the word "urgent," underlined in red. D'Agostino threw them in the trash.

His mother told him to go see Davio Giaccalone.

"Who told you about Davio?" he asked.

She shrugged. "I hear things," she said.

"Mom," he said, "you know what kind of person Davio is."

"He was a friend of Carmine's."

"There's no telling what he'll do."

"Well, I'm sorry," she said. "But sometimes you have to have a stomach for unpleasant things."

The crowds at the candlelight vigils grew. Sometimes there were more than one hundred people outside, chanting the Hail Mary as Rita Torresi led them through the rosary. They sang hymns and swayed from side to side, arms locked together. "Destroy this temple," Enzo raved through an amplified megaphone, "and in three days I will raise it up. . . ."

In the morning, after the six o'clock Mass, the old widows stayed to light candles to St. Anthony and the Blessed Mother, and when D'Agostino came out of the sacristy they flocked around him and said what a shame this whole thing was. He asked them to write letters to the cardinal. One of them looked up at him from under her shawl and said the cardinal was a tool of Satan. "Please," he said, "just write the letters. And be polite. Don't say anything about Satan."

He tried to accept the demolition as something inevitable. Things changed, he told himself; this was neither good nor bad. One morning he invited the engineers in for coffee, and when one of them apologized for what they were doing he smiled and explained that the church was not made up of buildings, but of people; that Mass could be said in a cave or a field. It didn't matter. The words, the beliefs, the rituals—these were what mattered, and these didn't change.

But on Friday afternoon, when James Keegan called to tell him about his new placement, all that philosophizing did him no good at all.

"It's good news and bad news," Keegan said.

"Just tell me."

"Michael." He cleared his throat. "You shouldn't have made the cardinal so angry."

"Just tell me. Good news first."

"It's in the United States."

D'Agostino's chest tightened. "And the bad?"

"Romulus, Michigan. It's near Detroit."

He felt as if he'd been kicked in the stomach. He sat down. For a moment he couldn't speak. Finally he said, "What about my mother?"

"Michael," Keegan said, "like I said, you shouldn't have got him so angry."

The best thing to do in the face of bad news was to pray. But he could not bring himself to kneel; what he wanted to do, in fact, was smash something. He walked upstairs to his room, then back downstairs to the kitchen. He opened a cabinet door and slammed it shut; the door bounced open and he slammed it shut again. He mixed a drink and threw it into the sink.

He had suffered for the church. He had spent two years in Bolivia, nine in Minneapolis, six in New Mexico, seven in Louisiana. Each year he had asked for a transfer to Massachusetts, so he could be near his mother. Now he would have to leave her again. He could not bear the thought of moving again, of starting a new life in some awful town in the middle of nowhere. He was old and tired and he did not have the energy for that anymore.

He put on his jacket, took his keys from the table, and drove to South Lawton.

Roy Maxwell was president of the Elks and although it was early in the afternoon it was clear that he had been drinking. His eyes were bloodshot and rimmed with red; there were patches of broken vessels in his nose and cheeks. They went out back to his office, a shabby little room with a suspended ceiling and wood paneling; there was a desk on one side, a cot on the other, and a pole with a dirty American flag leaning in the corner.

D'Agostino went into his pitch: all the men and women who

had worked to build that church, all the thousands of babies who had been baptized there, the couples who had been married there . . . but as he spoke he watched in amazement as Maxwell formed his thumb and forefinger into a beak and began to snap it open and shut.

"Yap, yap, yap, yap, yap," Maxwell said. He laughed. "You guys really know how to talk, don't you? Look, Father, nobody goes to that church anymore. You know that, and I know that. Whereas here, we got a hundred and seventy dues-paying members."

"That's hardly the point, Roy."

"Look, why're you putting up such a stink? You got some housewife you're banging? Or some altar boy?"

He drove off stunned and angry, the tires of his little Escort squealing and kicking up dirt in the Elks parking lot. Never in his life had he been insulted like that. And never before had he felt as desperate and full of rage. At Essex Street a woman cut across his lane and he hit his horn and threw her a gesture that he had not made since he was a boy. She looked at him, horrified; he remembered suddenly that he was wearing his Roman collar.

Something similar happened a few minutes later when he opened the door to Caffe Tripoli and stepped inside. The place went silent. The old men put down their cards. Davio Giaccalone, who was sitting at a table in back, stood up and blessed himself and said, "Father. Please, sit down."

D'Agostino was still seething from his encounter with Roy Maxwell. "No, thank you," he said.

They went for a walk. Friday evenings were busy in Little Italy; families crowded into the bakeries to buy pastries and bread for the weekend. Cars were doubled-parked on Common Street. Where, he wondered, were all these people on Sunday morning? He felt gloomy and cold.

"About this plan of yours," he said.

"Yes."

"I don't know why I even have to be involved. Why I have to be here."

Davio shrugged. "It's your church. You need a favor, I'm glad to do it."

He looked into Davio's eyes. They were black and deep and soulless. You could lose your soul for coveting earthly things, even if those things were good things. A church, a mother—they could cost you heaven. He did not know if that was what he was doing; but he thought it might be.

"Who else knows?"

"Nobody. You and me. No big deal."

"I don't want—" he said. But he couldn't finish.

"I know what you don't want," Davio said.

They shook hands. Then D'Agostino turned and hurried back up the street.

The Elks Club burned quickly and completely, and in the morning there was nothing left but the plumbing; the pipes stood against the sky like stick figures. D'Agostino saw the story and photograph in the Saturday paper. The fire had started in the middle of the night. Engines from three stations responded, but the building was gone before they got there.

When the four o'clock Mass was over he gathered up the remaining palm fronds and put them away in the sacristy, then drove to South Lawton to see for himself. There was nothing left but a mound of wet black ash through which a team of inspectors was digging. They stood knee-deep in the muck, blackened all over with wet soot. An ambulance and a fire engine and two police cruisers were parked nearby.

He parked near the cruisers and walked to where a small group was standing behind the police tape. He stood in the back, beside a thin man who was wearing a red ski parka and smoking a cigarette. Earlier in the day rain had fallen and now the air was cold and wet.

"What's this?" D'Agostino said, nodding toward the inspectors.

"They found a body," the man said. "The remains of one, anyway. Some guy was sleeping in there."

For a moment he felt nothing. Then his knees buckled underneath him. The horizon seemed to loom up and fall away, as if he were standing on a rolling ship. He thought he would faint; but he held himself. He mumbled something about feeling sick and retreated to his car. He drove toward his mother's house. The city seemed grotesque and exaggerated: warehouses and mills looming like flat black cutouts, garish neon signs throbbing in barroom windows, prostitutes huddled in doorways, bums in line outside the soup kitchen. He ran a red light, almost collided with a delivery truck, and turned up Haverhill Street toward Prospect Hill. He parked at the reservoir, beside a grove of pine trees above a cemetery. He stepped out of the car and felt his stomach kick and in a moment he was doubled over by the front tire, vomiting.

He walked to his mother's house. She met him on the porch. He told her about the body.

"It's been on the TV," she said.

They went to the kitchen. She made coffee, then sat and watched him stir sugar into his cup.

"He was an alcoholic," she said.

He didn't answer.

"And he was homeless. They let him sleep there sometimes. He was a single man, no wife or children. No family."

He got up and went to the couch. She turned on the television but he said, "No," and shut if off. He lay back, feeling as if life itself were draining out of him—wishing, in fact, that it would.

It wouldn't. Finally he got up and drove home and got into bed. He was unable to sleep. He began a rosary but he could not make himself pray. He closed his eyes and tried to confess, but it was as if he were speaking into a storm; the words spilled and scattered and blew away.

By five o'clock birds had begun to chitter in the trees. He dressed and walked to the church and offered Mass, barely hearing the words he spoke. It was Palm Sunday. He gave palm fronds to the man in the wheelchair and to the old widows, who smiled and blessed themselves when he spoke to them.

When he returned to the rectory Catalano was up making tea. The old man was humming to himself and poking through a cabinet over the sink. "I'm trying to find that honey," he said. "Didn't we buy some honey last week? I just had this urge to have honey in my tea. I can't find it anywhere."

At last Catalano gave up and had his tea with sugar. He made a cup for D'Agostino, who simply stared at the mug until the tea went cold.

The Sunday *Gazette* had a front-page story about the fire. A fire department investigator said there was no sign of foul play. In a separate story, Rita Torresi claimed the fire had been a miracle; Jesus, she said, had appeared to her in a dream Friday night, vowing to punish the Elks.

D'Agostino spent the week working in the garden. Peas and lettuce were enough to think about. On Monday he'd opened the *Gazette* and seen an obituary for the man killed in the fire, and this had sent his mind reeling. He asked Catalano to do the shopping. The old man gladly agreed; he seemed to have boundless energy these days. D'Agostino, on the other hand, was listless, ready to collapse, and he didn't dare venture beyond the walls of the courtyard.

On Tuesday James Keegan called to tell him, politely but abruptly, that the Elks had agreed to sell. "We hear you've been having miracles," he said. "We hope they cease soon."

"Me too," D'Agostino said.

But the story of the miracle gained force. A radio station put Rita Torresi on the air to discuss her dream and field questions from callers; people called in from as far away as Maine. The rectory phone rang constantly. D'Agostino let the calls go through to the machine, and erased the tape when it became full. He refused to give interviews. He would not even talk to his mother.

On Good Friday D'Agostino led the Stations of the Cross, and he could not remember when there had been so many people in the church. The aisles were packed. In the *Gazette* a man from New Hampshire speculated that a statue might bleed, or weep, or come to life: things like that really happened, the man said, and he wasn't going to miss it.

Enzo Russo came with his mother, and they walked with D'Agostino's mother, near the back of the procession. Near them were Rita Torresi and the rest of the Vita Dei group. After the service, D'Agostino saw Enzo and Rita moving through the crowd toward him; he ducked into the sacristy and stayed there until the church was empty.

Later, Catalano came into the rectory holding an envelope that contained ten one hundred dollar bills. "It was in the St. Anthony box," he said, trying to catch his breath. "It's incredible."

"I'm going to bed," D'Agostino said.

He went upstairs, his head pounding, his mouth dry, his heart racing in his chest. He hoped a heart attack might come and take him in the night. Instead he lay there, dizzy and aching. Waves of nausea washed over him. Catalano took all the Saturday Masses and came back raving about the crowds; in all his life he'd never seen anything like this, he said. D'Agostino groaned and went back to sleep.

The next morning, Easter Sunday, D'Agostino woke before dawn and felt fine. Whatever flu had gripped him had just as quickly let go. He dressed and walked to the church. He thought of the story he would read: the great stone rolled away from the tomb, Jesus sitting up and speaking. A chill came over him; suddenly he did not like being alone in the church.

But nothing happened. He filled the cruets and counted the hosts and said Mass. The statues did not move, the Holy Ghost did not appear; the burly man in the wheelchair sat in front, as always, and the three widows said their rosaries and paid no attention to D'Agostino. Again he thought: what a strange sight we must be.

At nine o'clock the pews were so crowded that people had to stand in the aisles. Cars were triple-parked on Common Street; the police sent an officer to write tickets and direct traffic. The Vita Dei people had collected money to buy lilies for the altar, and the church had the too-sweet flower smell that he associated with funerals. Marco DiMarca dusted off the organ in the balcony and played during both services, with his brother, Carlo, accompanying him on trumpet. Marco played as loud as the organ would go, and the great chords surged from the balcony like water crushing a dam.

Enzo and Rita and the rest of the Vita Dei group sat in a cluster on the left side of the church, near the statue of St. Anthony, to whom they gave credit for the miracle. D'Agostino's mother sat in the front row, in the same place where she sat every Sunday—the same place, in fact, where she'd watched him say his first Mass twenty-four years before.

He read the Gospel of John. The great old story: he'd spent his whole life telling it, but now he did not know if he believed it. If the story was true then he had lost his soul; if the story was false, he had wasted his life. The choice was a terrible one, and he was too confused now to decide. It would be a long time before he could be sure of anything.

He gave a sermon and led the hymns and recited the creed and not a single word meant anything to him; not a word. But during the consecration there was a great hushed energy, a tremendous force building. He felt this energy in his arms, his legs, the back of his neck. He held the chalice over his head and in the gold surface he saw a bent reflection of himself: his eyes wide, his head back, his hands reaching, his face distorted as if he were in pain. This, he thought, is the way God sees me.

Giancarlo,
for a Moment

GIANCARLO'S HANDS FLUTTER like little wings, propelling him. The smell of musk and lemons lingers as he passes. Darling, welcome, he says. Sit down, darling.

This is your day to become beautiful again.

You have a date tonight? Of course you do! How long is a woman like you going to stay unattached? And that what's-his-name? You forget his name already, am I right?

He hands you a magazine. You will wait for Giancarlo. But I'm worth the wait, no? He laughs and pets your hand and floats off to finish coloring the hair of a woman in a green linen summer dress. Darling, he calls her.

Just this morning he phoned and asked you to go to Prague with him.

"In Czechoslovakia?" you said.

"What," he said, "there's more than one?"

Think of Spain, he said. The Roman fortress in Antequera. The sun melting into the plain. "And Granada," he said. "You know what I'm talking about."

You did.

All he was saying, he said, was that you could travel together.

Like friends. Baby, he said. Honey. Sweetie, bunky, cha-cha. "Don't make me beg," he said.

Spain was a long time ago, you told him. And how many women had there been since then? Even when you were together, how many women had there been?

"OK," he said. "I'll beg."

He pushed you and you flew like a doll, weightless, against the counter. He shoved you out the door. He took your clothes and books and threw them onto the porch.

For a week you hated him. And then you went back. You averted your eyes and spoke in a near whisper. You said it had been your fault. You asked for another chance.

Your sister said this wasn't love. But whatever you felt for him, the name was not important. You felt it.

Just a tiny moment more, Giancarlo says. He holds his thumb and finger a fraction of an inch apart, like a bird's beak. He slips past as quick as a breeze. He lifts a strand of your hair and lets it drop. So fine, he says. So beautiful to work with.

You are reading an article about a woman who saved her daughter's life by having one of her kidneys removed and transplanted into the girl. You wonder if the middle-aged organ carried with it the foibles of middle age: Does the girl now avoid full-length mirrors? Does she complain that nobody around here appreciates her anymore? Does she want to go back and finish college, but not know what she wants to study? Does she wake up in the middle of the night and wish for the oblivion that lets men sleep?

Giancarlo is back, wiping his hands. Time to be beautiful! And you know the rules! You must tell me all about this new man, and I want details! Details, details!

*   *   *

51

You wanted to expand, you told him. To experiment. And so one time, after you knew him, you let him blindfold you and tie you to his bed. This was a thrill, exploring your dark corners. As a girl, you had searched the secret parts of your house: the eaves of the attic; the cool basement where the tools lay oily on the workbench; your father's closet, his wool suits ripe with the smell of sweat and cigars, the rows of shiny leather wingtips and loafers, a shoe box full of letters.

Over time there was more. You were on your hands and knees in the hallway; you were wearing stockings he gave you—"a gift," he said, and you took them that way. He slapped you as you came, until you needed the one to have the other. You came like never before, in wide incessant waves that curled and hovered impossibly before the splash and collapse.

You trusted him. You told yourself what he told you, that all this was within a circumference of love. He explained the paradox of submission: that the submissive, by remaining passive, is actually in control. This made you feel better. You believed him.

So, *bella*, the full treatment, yes? Giancarlo holds his fingers at the base of your neck. There is a tiny charge when the fingers move across your skin. His hair is oiled and pulled back from his face. In the mirror he is taller, thinner, darker. You, however, are gaunt and pale and waxy: a cancer victim, a bag lady, an inmate in a psychiatric unit—the "before" photo in *Cosmopolitan*.

How, you wonder, have you let your hair get this long? Have you been asleep all these months? And if you have been sleeping, why do you look like someone who hasn't slept?

You recline, and Giancarlo cradles the nape of your neck. The first water scorches your scalp—you tighten, but you don't complain.

So, *bella*, you have to tell me everything about him, that's our deal. A pilot? For an airline? Delta? And he's handsome? Of course! It's a job requirement, did you know that? Yes! They've all had plastic surgery, it's wonderful!

Giancarlo's fingers skip up the back of your neck, your secret spot. You tingle. You are suddenly aware of your breasts. A wisp of hair snags on his finger and there is a tug, then a tear. You tighten.

Did I hurt you, he says.

You shake your head.

Then relax, *bella!* I'm not a woman hater! He jabs his fingers back into the wet nest of your hair.

When you were about to come he would weave his fingers into the hair at the back of your neck and as you began to cry out he would pull, and suddenly your scalp would come alive with a million dots of fire and your neck would arch back, exposing your throat.

Giancarlo moves the comb slowly through your wet hair and again there are snags, tiny bites, and again you do not complain. You smell lemons and you remember when you were a girl and everything came in lemon scent—shampoo, air freshener, dish-washing liquid. That was the thing then.

Do you know, he says, that all the pilots have perfect vision? Yes! They have to! Twenty-twenty or they're out! So we'll give Mr. Delta something for his eyes, then.

He holds his hand flat, like a karate chop, by the side of your neck. About here? Higher? Here? More? *Bella,* you'll look like a boy!

But you don't want your hair. You do not want any part of you that is from that old time.

Bella, he says. He makes a sad clown face.

That's what I want, you say.

He pretends to be angry. He picks up his scissors and begins to cut. Maybe you want to be bald, then, he says.

When he asked to shave you, you didn't know what he meant at first. Then he showed you pictures. Strange, the folds of skin. Like a tire with the air let out.

The water was warm and the shaving cream felt like silk; you moved your hips for his hand. Then, for the razor, you held still. He was careful. He took a long time. Afterward he held a mirror and there you were, a girl again: you nearly fainted. Then, at the first touch of his mouth, you actually did faint, for a second.

In July he phoned and asked you to go to Peru. "The Andes," he said. "A two-day train ride to Bolivia. Altitude sickness."

You admitted that it did sound perfect. You reminded him, though, that the last time you'd visited you had left a day early. So what had changed? And where had he been all these months? "You just vanish, and then you pop up and ask me to travel to the other side of the earth," you said.

He didn't respond.

"Hello?" you said.

"Temperatures," he said, "are below freezing at night."

You asked him what that had to do with anything.

Klaus Barbie, he said, had hidden in La Paz after the war. "Imagine the kind of place it must be."

You could think of nothing to say.

"Am I pissing into the wind here?" he said. "Is it hopeless? Because I know you still love me. We're made for each other. Yin and yang. We fit."

You couldn't help yourself. You laughed.

Suddenly your face is wider and your eyes are farther apart. You look like a poster child. Well, I warned you, Giancarlo says.

Giancarlo, for a Moment

You are crying. He rushes away and returns with Kleenex. He glances around the room. He does not want a scene. *Bella, bella,* he says. You look . . . innocent. You look wonderful. It's not that, you tell him.

He stands behind you and runs his hands through your little boy's haircut. He peppers you with compliments. Somewhere behind you a woman is talking about her husband. "Oh, he's a *bastard.*" She laughs. "I'm telling you, he's such a *bastard!*"

Giancarlo gives you advice about your pilot. He tells you tricks to keep from being nervous. You nod and pretend that he's helping you. You imagine your pilot tonight: the awkward conversation, the realization that even though you asked, you really don't care where he's been.

At the party last week, you noticed that the wind did not lift the pilot's hair, and you became suspicious. Implants? A weave? He told you that he lived in the South End. "It's all fags there now," he said. "They're always hitting on me. I hate that."

Even then, as you regarded his tan and wondered whether he'd got it in a salon, you knew that he would ask for your number. You knew he would call you, and that you would accept. Even then, fifteen minutes after meeting him, you noticed that he poured his beer into a glass and you could imagine him in bed: earnest, on top of you, his head buried into the pillow, his breath in your ear—afterward you would smile and say it was nice, and he would turn his handsome, satisfied face toward you for a moment before falling asleep. In the morning, after he left, you would draw a bath and curl yourself up under the faucet and imagine yourself in Lima.

He had pimples on his back, and his eyes were too small and too far apart, but he knew you so well that at times you thought he *was* you. You told him everything. The cousin who took you to bed. The dyke in college, her hot mouth on you. He peeled you and never looked away. Nothing was too bad for him.

Once, home from a nightclub, brain-dead from Quaaludes and dancing, you fell asleep while fucking. Hours later, with the day stretching into afternoon, you woke still locked together and simply began fucking again, as if you'd never slept, as if time did not exist.

Giancarlo gels your hair. The strands shine like tiny glass pipettes. He wipes his hands on a towel, but as he brings them back across your face there is a trace of lemon odor there. Two chairs down, a girl is singing with the radio: *Open your heart to me* . . .

Giancarlo raves about your pilot. He's going to love you! He'll be all over you!

You smile. You realize, dreadfully, that he's right.

You say, Giancarlo, you don't understand.

What don't I understand?

This date is useless, you say. It will not amount to anything. The pilot is never going to be my boyfriend, you tell him. You're beginning to cry again.

Ah, *bella.* Of course he won't be your boyfriend! And do you know why? No? Because Giancarlo is your boyfriend! Yes, that's right! For this moment, Giancarlo is your boyfriend. Close your eyes. That's it. You feel my fingers? Good, eh? You like it here? Here? Over here? Softer, like this? Slower? In circles? Up and down? You love me? Do you? Say it! Of course you do! And I love you!

You open your eyes. Staring out from the mirror is some weird tomboy flapper, some girl from a Fitzgerald story. Once, in high school, a friend talked you into getting a permanent, and even that did not look this stupid. You are twenty-eight years old, weeping in a hair salon. This is not what your life was supposed to be. You still want him—him and his meanness, him and his crazy vacations.

Beneath the flapper's haircut is not some new person. It's you. Your face, your eyes, your heart. You think of your heart. You remember the little girl with the transplant, and you realize that's what you need: a new heart! But not your mother's—no, you would want the heart of a girl, with its muscles still strong, its chamber walls still not tainted by the sour flow of love.

But of course this is impossible. And it is not love that has stained your heart. Love is a foreign language, one that you do not yet understand. When you step out into Newbury Street the bright sun hurts your eyes.

The Greyhound

WHAT WE STOLE was a greyhound. Her name was Coco and she belonged to Davio Giaccalone, the president of the local chapter of the Ladies Garment Workers Union. Giaccalone was a dime-store mafioso, a fat old man who wore sweaty suits and sharp-toed shoes and who supposedly once had snipped off the thumbs of a driver who'd stolen a few cartons of cigarettes from one of his trucks.

That story about the thumbs was the first thing my roommate Evan and I learned when we moved to Little Italy. The second thing we learned was that everyone hated us. We couldn't leave because we'd signed a one-year lease ("Old World charm," the ad said), and so there we were, two white male oppressors trapped in the land of the swarthy people.

Giaccalone's racing dog was as skinny as a runway model, with a face like Sophia Loren's and eyes like big saucers of milk, and when she walked down Newbury Street I swear those foolish guineas would stand aside and start to whisper. Coco had been a big champion at Seabrook and Wonderland. I won ninety dollars on her once, before Giaccalone took her in payment of a gambling debt and made her sit by his Caffe Tripoli table like a slave begging bits of pastry from his hand.

"It's disgusting," I said, as Coco snapped a piece of chocolate-covered pizzelli from Giaccalone's hand, which glittered with gold rings the size of walnuts. "A dog like that, a racing dog—you can't keep it as a pet."

"What," Evan said, "they should build it a shrine?"

Evan is a software programmer, like me, and like me he is not a geek. He reads Freud and Campbell and cyberpunk novels, and once at a party I saw him drive an earnest, hairy-legged Cambridge girl to tears by insisting that he no longer believed in anything. The next morning I came into the living room and found her sitting on the couch wearing Evan's Star Trek T-shirt and drinking a cup of coffee.

"I won ninety dollars on that dog once," I told him.

"You thought I forgot since the last time you told me?"

I called for our bill and sure enough the waiter tried to cheat us; he'd charged us four dollars instead of three.

"Amigo," I said.

"That's Spanish," Evan said.

"Whatever. Hey. Waiter."

He came back, pretended he didn't speak English, and insisted we pay the four bucks. I tried to make myself clear: "Blow me," I said.

Meanwhile, Giaccalone had turned in his chair and was taking an interest. The waiter ran over and whispered to him, and then the old bastard started calling us faggots and had his nephew, Tony, throw us out.

We went to the beach and got wasted on Fog Cutters. When we got back every parking space in Little Italy was taken, and so I moved the barrels out of the space reserved for Giaccalone's Fleetwood and put my Toyota there.

"To hell with him," I said. "I live here too."

"I love it when you get all drunk and Catholic and indignant," Evan said.

We staggered up the four flights to our apartment and crashed out. In the morning, when I stepped outside to get the newspaper, I found the Corolla slumped onto the pavement, with all its tires slashed.

Giaccalone said he didn't know anything about any tires on any faggot's car. The waiters stood behind the counter, washing dishes. The old guineas in back looked up from their game of dominoes, then kept playing.

"So nobody here saw anyone near my car," I said.

"Nobody here saw nothing," Giaccalone said.

The desk cop at the police station—whose name was *Incorpora*, which is, of course, an Italian name—gave me a report to fill out and said there was nothing they could do. I asked why they couldn't look around a little, maybe pressure an informer. "What do you think this is?" he said. "Starsky and Hutch?"

That afternoon, when a crew from the garage came to replace the tires, a crowd gathered on the sidewalk and Mrs. Migliore, our neighbor from across the hall, clucked her tongue and shook her head and whispered to the other old ladies in Sicilian.

"What could you possibly have been thinking?" said Maria Mendez, the Puerto Rican girl who worked in the laundry on the first floor of our building.

I wanted to tell her that in any other city, in any other neighborhood, this would not have happened. Nowhere in America, I wanted to say, would a greasy, shit-filled crispelli like Davio Giaccalone be allowed to tyrannize a neighborhood. But it was a hot day, I was still woozy from the Fog Cutters, and there was no use making speeches.

"It was late," I told her. "I was tired."

"And drunk, too, probably." She smiled and pulled her curly brown hair away from her face. "You Irish, you shouldn't drink."

The Greyhound

Maria was wearing a pair of cut-offs, and the puffy white crescents of her ass peeked out beneath the fringe. I thought again about asking her out. She worked for the guy who owned our building, and every once in a while she'd sneak out and come up to our place for a cup of tea. One time I'd made plans to have dinner with her, but then I found out she had a daughter, so I canceled. Told her I had the flu. But now, with my car up on jacks and my luck running off in a dozen crazy directions, I saw in Maria the promise of a sane life; I saw Sunday dinners and afternoon screwing, a little bedroom with floral wallpaper and a crucifix hanging over the door. I pulled Evan over beside the tow truck and asked him if he thought she'd give me another chance. "Give me some advice," I said.

Evan adjusted his glasses and eyed the crowd. "Move your car," he said.

For days I paced back and forth between the kitchen and living room, cooking up schemes for revenge. The good plans, like smashing the windows in Giaccalone's Fleetwood, were too dangerous. The safe ones, like waking Giaccalone with phone calls in the middle of the night, were so silly that to carry them out would only humiliate me further.

One Friday night we were out on the fire escape with a bottle of White Label when we saw a dog wandering down Newbury Street, poking her nose into the trash bags on the sidewalk.

"Is that Coco?" I said.

"No," Evan said, "it's the world's tallest rat."

"Fucking Giaccalone. The guy should be shot. A dog like that, out eating garbage."

"Someone should give her a good home," Evan said.

I smiled at him. He smiled at me. And before we knew it we'd run downstairs and opened the door and then Coco was in our apartment, wolfing a piece of New York strip that we diced up and placed in a soup bowl for her. She darted around the apartment, sniffing at the furniture. Then, without so much as a whimper, she curled up in an armchair and fell asleep.

I balanced myself on the arm of the chair and stroked her neck. "The great Coco," I said.

Evan lay on the couch. "The great Coco," he muttered. "Did I tell you I once won ninety dollars on this dog?"

He began to snore.

I lay on my bed in my shorts. "Ninety dollars."

Next morning, same as ever, the white cups gleamed in their racks behind the counter at Caffe Tripoli, the pastries lay in rows in the cases, and the air had that wonderful, bitter taste of espresso.

But anyone could see that something terrible had happened to Giaccalone. There were dark circles around his eyes. His hair had not been combed. He was chain-smoking. He ignored his sweet roll and coffee. He picked up the paper and put it down, then sat wringing his hands like a zombie and looking out the window.

Tony ran in and whispered in his uncle's ear. The old man said something. Tony shook his head. The old man cuffed him and said, "Then try again," and Tony ran out.

I held the *Gazette* up in front of my face. "This is better than sex," I said.

"I can't remember what sex feels like."

"Like your hand, only warmer. You think he suspects us?"

Evan stirred sugar into his cappucino. "This guy couldn't suspect his way out of a broom closet."

We brought a cannoli home for Coco. She met us at the door, wagging her tail. "Look, she actually likes this dump," Evan said.

She had finished the bacon and eggs that I'd put out for her, and there was a fresh loaf of dog crap on the newspaper under the kitchen table. I rolled up the paper, tossed it in the trash, and set out a fresh sheet.

Evan bent over. "Wait a minute—is this my mother's soup bowl? A dog is eating out of my mother's china?"

"Relax. A dog's mouth is way cleaner than a human's. Everybody knows that."

"I don't know that." He picked up the bowl and put it into the sink.

There was a knock at the door. I looked out the peephole. Mrs. Migliore was in the hallway, craning her neck up at me.

"Christ," I said, "it's the Bride of Frankenstein again."

"Has she got Gus with her?"

"No," I said.

Gus DeSanto, the neighborhood plumber, visited the Bride two or three times a week. He carried his toolbox, as if he had come to fix something, and in a way I guess he had, because he always came out after an hour or so with his hair messed up and a spring in his step.

"What the hell does she want?" Evan said.

"What, I'm a mind reader? Get the dog out of here."

She knocked again.

I said, "Just a minute."

"It's Mrs. Migliore. I need to talk to you."

"OK," I said. "Just a minute."

Evan took Coco into his room. "Ask her if she's wearing underwear," he said.

"You boys were playing that music again last night." She spidered into the living room. "I asked you not to play that music."

"That's a nice dress, Mrs. Migliore."

She clicked her tongue against her teeth, then spied the newspaper on the floor. "You have a pet?"

"Our pipes leak. Maybe you could send Gus over, next time he's here."

She scowled. "There are no pets here. They bring fleas."

"We don't have a pet."

"You've heard about Mr. Giaccalone's dog?"

I shook my head. "You mean Coco?"

"Gone." The old lady nodded.

"The people from the race track took her?"

She peered up at me through her thick glasses, which magnified her eyes and made her look like a creature from outer space. "Where is your roommate?"

"Doing errands. I was just running out myself."

I opened the door. She began to step out, then stopped and wagged her finger. "Pets bring fleas," she said.

The original plan was to hold Coco hostage for the weekend, just long enough to put old Giaccalone into the cardiac unit at Lawton Falls General. But on Sunday morning I opened the *Gazette* and found he'd placed an ad offering a $5,000 reward for the return of his dog.

"Well, folks," I said, "it's a whole new ballgame."

Evan, of course, had to pretend that he had morals. It's a Jewish thing, King Solomon and all that. Catholics, we just swing away, like Wade Boggs with a three-and-one-count, and when the sinning's done we go to confession and have our souls wiped clean.

"I don't know," he said. "I mean, it's one thing to pull a hack, but this—this would be stealing."

I reminded him that I'd gone along with his idea to put the Jerusalem B virus in the sales department's computers, and that I'd shared the blame with him when he couldn't clear it from the server. "You owe me," I said. "Besides, the guy ruined my car. He owes me for those tires."

"What if they catch us? They'll cut off our thumbs. How do you type without thumbs?"

"You tap the space bar with your stump."

In the end he came around. I knew he would. He wanted to do it as much as I did. Who wouldn't? The clincher was when I reminded him that his $3,200 VISA balance was going to cost him $576 in interest alone this year. "You pay it off, you can start all over again," I said.

"OK, OK, I'm in," he said. Now that we were partners he was all excited. "The whole neighborhood's talking about it," he said. "They've got posters up everywhere, and they've got all the little kids out hunting around. It's crazy. By the way, I saw Maria."

"Did she say anything about me?"

"Yeah, let me see," he said. "She said you're a fag and you wear your pants too high."

"Blow me."

"I'm off baby food."

We rented post office boxes in Edmunds, Newburyport, and Boston, all under false names, and arranged to have the mail to the Boston box forwarded to Edmunds, and the mail to Edmunds forwarded to Newburyport. This was my plan. "Clean, simple, elegant," I said.

Evan smirked. "Childish, low-tech, thoroughly unworkable."

"Hey," I said, "we're not dealing with rocket scientists here."

But when we called Giaccalone's reward hotline and Evan said, in his "Squeaky the Clown" falsetto voice, that we wanted the money mailed to us, the guy laughed. "It's those kids again," he said. "Hey, mail *this*, motherfucker." Then he hung up.

"Look," Evan said, "why don't we just take the dog down there, tell them we found her, and collect the money?"

"Golly, Evan, why don't we jump in front of trucks on Route

93? Why don't we wander around Roxbury late at night? They won't pay us—they'll kill us."

He lay down on the couch and adjusted his glasses, which he'd repaired with black electrical tape so that they made him look like someone who'd escaped from an asylum. Which was appropriate, since outside our little hostage den the whole city was going crazy.

On Broadway, on Essex Street, on the door of the Hibernians—the whole downtown was papered with Coco posters, and up on Prospect Hill little packs of children spent their evenings running through the backyards calling for Coco. Reward posters filled the grocery store windows; the ushers at Holy Trinity handed them out at Mass stapled to the parish bulletin. At night, Gus DeSanto snuck down the alley behind our building, calling to the dog, then ran up the backstairs and gave the Bride the high hard one.

On Wednesday Giaccalone raised the reward to $10,000, and the *Gazette* ran a story on the front page with a picture of the old crook holding a framed photograph of Coco and looking distraught. The headline read, "Lost Dog Brings $10,000 Reward; 'She's Like My Child,' Cafe Owner Says."

"*Cafe owner?* That's like calling Charles Manson a youth club director," I said.

"I didn't know he owned the cafe."

"Christ only knows what he owns." I tossed the paper onto the coffee table. "Anyway, ten thousand bucks. I feel like goddamn Julius Rosenberg."

"What?"

"You know, with the Lindbergh baby. Julius and Ethel Rosenberg."

"The Rosenbergs didn't steal the Lindbergh baby."

"Well, that's what you say. But from what I've read there was proof."

"The Rosenbergs were convicted of spying."

"What?"

"It was a different case. The Lindbergh baby was someone else."

"Well, whatever." I picked up the paper. "That's what I feel like."

"You're going to feel like Jimmy Hoffa if we wait much longer."

Coco was not just a dog; she was the uber-pet. So I hated the fact that we had to keep her cooped up. She had way too much dignity for that. Take the TV controller. She knew that when I watched TV I didn't play with her, so she used to hide the controller, and only after I'd played with her for a while would she lead me to it. I had nine credits toward a master's degree and this *dog* was teaching me tricks. And then, as if to insult me, right in the middle of playing she'd drop into an armchair and fall asleep, and I'd be standing there with a chew toy in my hand, feeling like a fool.

She'd been spoiled. When we brought her bones from the butcher in Reading, or toys from the pet store at the mall, when we covered her armchair with a comforter, when we gave her one of my Converse All-Stars to chew—never, not once, did she show any appreciation. She used our gifts and played our fetch game and let us pet her, but she kept us at a distance. I was never sure whether she loved us or despised us.

"She reminds me of a girl I went out with in college," Evan said. "Beth Heidelman, from Shaker Heights. Total JAP."

"Be serious," I said. "You went out with a girl in college?"

Like fools, we competed for her affection. We fed her steak at night, bacon and eggs in the morning, and at lunch we took turns driving home to feed her hamburger and give her fresh water. It was sick. A lot of times I'd stop on the way and pick up a cannoli, just so I could stand there, enraptured, and watch as she snapped up the chunks of ricotta cheese with her long, muscled tongue.

At night when we got home she met us at the door. We started calling her the Wife. She watched movies with us on the VCR, she hid behind the armchair and peeked out, and at night, if she slept in Evan's room, I felt—well, I felt jealous.

We worked at a place called Ionic Software Corp., developing (I use the term loosely) a groupware program called Nectar. The project was two years past deadline, the fake-tan assholes in marketing were screaming for code, and we were nowhere near done. The thing was crawling with bugs; every time we fixed one we created two. It was insane. We'd long ago decided that Nectar would never actually work, and that we were simply biding time until marketing caught on and fired us. "Who gives a shit about groupware, anyway?" Evan used to say. "I mean, why do these people want to work in groups in the first place?"

Now, with a dog held hostage in our apartment and the mob ready to drill us new assholes, neither of us could concentrate long enough to even look for bugs in Nectar, let alone fix them. Evan spent his days going for coffee and hovering around the girls in the sales department. I played video games, and in the evening I found excuses to visit Maria at the laundry.

"We've got a pool going," she said. "Pick the day that Coco comes back and you win the money."

"What if she doesn't come back?"

"We give the money to the church. We're selling Coco T-shirts, too." She held up a shirt with a picture of Coco and the words *Have You Seen Me?* silk-screened on the front. "Blue or white. Ten dollars. You want one?"

I bought two—white, extra large—and brought them upstairs and showed them to Evan. "This whole neighborhood is out of its mind," I said.

He was in his bedroom at his computer, trading E-mail on one of the X-rated bulletin boards. Coco was asleep on the bed, muzzled and leashed to a bedpost.

"Look at this shit," he said.

I leaned over and read the semi-coherent ravings of some fool talking to a woman named Gloria about his hard-on, and following her orders to put an ice cube up his ass.

"Who are these sick fucks?"

"The guy is an account executive in New York."

"What about Gloria?"

"*C'est moi.*"

"What?"

A line appeared on the screen: WHAT SHOULD I DO NEXT.

Evan typed: TAKE A PAPERCLIP AND CLIP IT TO YOUR RIGHT NIPPLE. THEN DO THE LEFT.

A line appeared: YOU'RE VICIOUS, GLORIA.

Evan typed: THAT'S MISTRESS GLORIA TO YOU, SCUM.

"This is disgusting," I said. "Even for you."

"Last week I made him singe the hair off his balls with a lighter."

A line appeared: I'M BLEEDING . . .

I flipped off the computer, grabbed Evan by the shoulder, and reminded him that we might be bleeding ourselves, and bleeding profusely at that, if we didn't come up with a way to ransom back the dog.

"Fuck off," he said. "You're the mastermind here."

The first thing we had to do, I said, was show our faces in Caffe Tripoli. "We can't stop going," I said. "If we do we'll look like suspects."

"Good thinking, Raskolnikov," Evan said.

No sooner had we found a table and ordered coffee than Tony appeared at our table. "Hello, ladies," he said. "How're those new tires?"

"Great," I said. "How's the missing dog?"

He snickered. "Why, you got her? You fucking her in the ass? You're sick of doing it to each other, is that it?"

"You sound jealous."

For a moment he stood there, turning his pinkie ring. I thought maybe he was getting ready to hit one of us. But then he said, "You know what I think?"

"I didn't know you did think," I said.

"I think you wouldn't know what to do with that dog, because it's a girl."

"Tony," Evan said, "what *is* that perfume you're wearing?"

We were in the lab at work, reading other people's E-mail messages off the server, when the solution came to me.

"Evan," I said, as we closed another of the pathetic love letters that our boss McGill had been sending to one of the sales assistants, "can you hack into a bank?"

"Depends. If it's a 3090, like at Mass Bank, sure."

"You can get in and get out?"

"Reilly," he said, "on a 3090 I'm Jesus Christ. I can walk on water, OK?"

I switched on his modem. "Then start dialing," I said. "I'll make coffee."

After three hours of screwing up, we tapped into the Mass Bank host system. We created a new account, using the name Gloria Domina; we gave her a balance of $250. The next day I went to the branch office on Newbury Street. "I'd like to make a deposit into my wife's account," I said. "I don't have her passbook."

"No problem," the girl said.

She called up the Gloria Domina account, took my $100, and handed me a receipt that showed a $350 balance. "Have a nice day," I said, and after I walked out Evan walked in and opened an account in his name.

That night we called Giaccalone's hotline. I listened on the extension; Evan did the talking. "Don't hang up," he squeaked. "We're serious."

"All right, Tinkerbell," the guy said. "There's a track number tattooed in the dog's left ear. Tell me the number."

Evan looked down the hall at me. His eyes were as wide as two big moons. He mouthed the word, "Tattoo?"

I looked in and sure enough there was a number, in blue ink, across the inside of Coco's ear. I wrote the number on a piece of paper and held it up so he could see it.

"Seven three three seven," he said.

"Shit." He rustled a piece of paper. "OK, what's in the other ear?"

I wrote the word "fleas" and held the paper up to Evan. He threw me the finger and mimed, "Come on."

I checked, and held up the paper again.

"Seven nine A," Evan said.

The guy took a deep breath and said, "OK, pal, you bring us the dog, we pay you the money. It's as simple as that."

"It's not that simple. Get out a paper and pencil, and I'm going to give you a name and a bank account number where I want you to deposit the money."

"You're not going to pull this shit again, are you?"

Evan gave me his little-kid-lost-in-the-mall look; I couldn't take it anymore.

"Look, jerky," I said, "the dog hasn't eaten in three days. You make us wait another and we're going to turn her into hamburger."

"Who was that?"

"Nobody," Evan squeaked. He waved at me to shut up. "But . . . but we'll do what he said. We'll do it, believe me."

"Hold a minute." The man went off the line; when the line opened again Giaccalone was speaking.

"I want to hear her bark," he said.

"You what?"

"Bark, dick-breath. How do I know she's still alive? Make her bark."

I took off Coco's muzzle, wrapped my arm around her and pinched her, hard, in the neck. She yelped.

"All right, you sick fucks. Give me the account number. And if we don't see that dog by tomorrow night, we go to the bank and freeze the account. And then we come looking for you."

"It's Mass Bank," Evan said. "The name is Gloria Domina. D-O-M-I-N-A. The account number is one-one-two-one-three-seven-five."

"Domina?" he said. "Isn't that the broad who goes out with Angiulo? Hey, who is this? Is this the fucking Angiulos?"

"Just make the deposit."

"Hamburger?" Evan said. "We're going to turn her into hamburger?"

"I had to get his attention."

"You're a deviant, Reilly. A complete and utter deviant."

At ten thirty the next morning we tapped into the Mass Bank system. Gloria's balance was $10,350.

"I could cry," I said.

Evan transferred the money to his account, and we drove to the Mass Bank branch at the mall and withdrew the money. We went back to work looking as if nothing had happened, which is not an easy thing to do when you're carrying $10,350 in cash in your backpack. We tapped into the Mass Bank system again. We vaporized Gloria Domina, and closed Evan's account.

"No fingerprints," I said. "No paper trail."

"So how do we get rid of the dog?"

"Piece of cake."

"Really? How?"

"Don't worry."

"Don't worry? Don't worry? What—you don't have a plan?"

"I have a plan," I said. "It's in the gestation phase."

The problem, of course, was the Bride. She ran to her peephole whenever anyone so much as moved in the hallway. There was no way to get the dog out past her.

"We could wait until three in the morning," Evan said.

"Too risky. She might be up soaking her hemorrhoids or something."

We went home and sat in the apartment and tried to come up with something. Down on Newbury Street a couple of Giaccalone's thugs were standing on the sidewalk in leather jackets and driving gloves, scanning the street like Secret Service men.

"By now they've been to the bank," I said. "They know the money's gone."

Evan let the curtain fall back across the window. "I can't believe I let you talk me into this." Coco pressed her face against his cheek and tried to lick him through her muzzle, but he pushed her away. "Fuck off," he said, then went to his room.

I sat down; I stood up. I lay on the couch. But for the life of me I couldn't think of a way to get that dog out of the building. We might still be taking care of her today if Gus DeSanto hadn't come poking along after dark, calling to Coco in the alley behind our building.

"Out looking for Coco again?" I asked as he skipped up onto our landing with a flashlight in his hand.

"For ten thousand bucks? You bet. And, well, Lucia's been having some trouble with her kitchen sink, so since I was going by. . . ."

The Bride opened her door and glared at him. "Mr. Reilly has been having trouble with leaks in his apartment, too," she said. "Maybe you should have a look over there, too."

"Ours seems to have taken care of itself."

"Good, then." She yanked the poor sap into her kitchen.

I ran to Evan's room. "T minus ten minutes and counting," I said. "Get your big raincoat, put it over the dog, and wait here."

I ran downstairs to the laundry. Maria Mendez was getting ready to close up for the night.

"Maria, it's an emergency," I said. "Do you still have the pass key for the apartments?"

"No, it grew legs and ran away." She reached up and took the key from a nail on the wall behind her. "What's the matter? You lock yourself out again?"

"It's Mrs. Migliore. We heard a crash, and then she was making, like, this moaning sound, and then there wasn't any sound at all."

"Jesus Christ," she said, then blessed herself and ran up the stairs behind me.

We stood outside the Bride's door. "Hear anything?" I whispered.

"I hear a noise." She leaned closer. "There it is again."

I opened my door. "You go in," I said. "I'm going to call an ambulance."

We were down the stairs and opening the backdoor for Coco when the shouting began. The Bride was screaming in Italian, Maria was screaming back in Spanish—God knows what they were saying—and by the time Gus came flying down the backstairs, with his T-shirt on and his pants unbuttoned, Coco had raced down the alley and out of sight.

"How're those pipes, Gus," I said.

"Fuck you," he said, then ran off.

For a moment we stood looking at each other and not talking; it was one of those fine, clear times when your heart seems to open up and everything good about life rushes in.

"Come on," Evan said. "Let's get wasted."

We drank champagne, we ate lobsters, and we put caviar on

crackers which, after I tasted one, I threw into the sink. Evan did his impersonation of Tony. We threw the money around like confetti. We drank a bottle of Madeira, a bottle of armagnac, and I got so loaded that at one point I was going to light a Macanudo with a $100 bill before Evan stopped me.

"A toast," I said, lifting a glass of port. "Good guys one, guineas nothing."

Then I passed out. When I woke it was the next morning and I was lying beneath a blanket of bills, like a kid in a leaf pile. The room was strewn with ashtrays and bottles and empty boxes, and there was a smell of smoke and food gone bad. My mouth tasted like I'd been eating garbage. Outside a truck groaned in the alley. The sun laid a pale line along the tops of the buildings across the street; the light was still too thin to warm the air, and the room seemed dead, like a beach the day after a storm.

"Evan," I said.

He turned, but didn't answer. He lay on the couch with a newspaper over his face, which was just as well, I thought, because what I wanted to say might be embarrassing. I lay on the floor, unable to sit up: to move was to feel my brain slosh across my head and collide with the side of my skull.

"You know, I was thinking I might take my money and open a little restaurant. You know? Like a breakfast place."

"Reilly," he said, "fuck off."

I tried to sit up, but the room tilted and spun like a carnival ride and I had to lie back down. "Also," I said, "I'm going to ask Maria Mendez out. I'm going to make a life for myself."

"I'm going to puke," Evan said, then dragged himself off to the bathroom.

I listened to him retching, then drifted back toward sleep. Outside in the street a man was singing while he unloaded a truck, and a boy was calling his friends out to play. Birds sang on the phone wires.

I woke to the sound of a dog barking in the street. The barking was close. I opened my eyes. Evan was standing at the window, looking down at the street. He seemed as if he might get sick again.

There was pounding on the door. "Open up," Mrs. Migliore said. "Somebody wants to see you."

My head felt as if it might split open. "Say it ain't so," I said.

But Coco kept howling and throwing herself at the door, Mrs. Migliore continued to knock, and I, flat on my back, felt weightless and empty, as if my heart had stopped beating. Evan fell onto the couch, face down. From the street came the sound of slapping footsteps, and men swearing in Italian.

I reached for the phone and managed to knock the earpiece out of its cradle. I dialed zero; there was nothing. I clicked, then clicked again. The line was dead.

All Best Wishes

THE LETTER was made out to Rebecca, and had no return address. Martin separated the mail into two piles—his, hers—and placed this letter at the top of her stack. The envelope was white, with a fold in the middle, as if it had been carried in a pocket. The postmark was from Worcester, three days before. On the back there was a fine brown crescent where someone had put down a coffee mug, then wiped away the stain. The address was written in blue ink, in a man's handwriting.

In the entire world, Martin knew, there was only one man that Rebecca had loved before him. This man's name was Tyler, and he had left Rebecca for another woman. He and the woman now lived somewhere in western Massachusetts. Rebecca insisted that she hated Tyler.

He sat down on the couch to open his mail. There was a fund-raising plaint from his college, which he opened and put with the electric bill. There was a postcard with a picture of a missing boy, offering a reward. There was a coupon book, a flyer from Stop & Shop, and a letter from American Express offering travel insurance. All these he threw into the trash.

Their house was a small ranch in a neighborhood of small ranches, and it was not their house, really. They rented. Home prices were reasonable in Lawton Falls, even for newspaper reporters—most of the other people at the *Gazette* owned houses—but for Martin and Rebecca it was out of the question. "It's too complicated," Rebecca said. At one time they had talked about marriage; but now they avoided the subject.

When she got home he told her about the letter.

"Really?" she said. "How mysterious."

He handed her the envelope. Her eyes widened for an instant.

"Who's it from?" he said.

"Well, I don't know, do I?" Rebecca was from England, and she had a way of talking down to people. She riffled through her other letters.

"You don't know?"

"Martin," she said, "I'm not a mind reader."

She walked to the kitchen. He followed her. She put her mail on the cutting block, opened the refrigerator, and took out the pitcher of iced tea.

"Aren't you going to open it?"

She took a glass from the cabinet and filled it with iced tea. She put the pitcher back.

"Are you going to read it?"

"Of course I am. Of course I'm going to read it."

He looked at the envelope. "Well?"

"Martin." She put her hand on the stack of envelopes. "This is my mail. *Mine.*"

"We don't have any secrets, do we?"

"Of course not, love. I'm not Susan, am I?" She leaned out and kissed him on the lips.

"We agreed we wouldn't talk about her," he said.

"Well, I'm just saying." She waved her hand over the mouth of a brown paper grocery bag like a magician. "Nothing up my sleeve," she said. Then she reached in, lifted out a jar of green paste and said, "Pesto!"

Martin picked up the *Gazette* and went out to the back porch.

A few minutes later she came outside with her mail and her iced tea. Martin sat on a chaise longue, pretending to read, and he watched her open her letters. Next door, mosquitoes snapped into the bug light in Mrs. Carlson's yard. Finally the only letter left was the one from Worcester. Rebecca picked it up, then said, "Oh," as if she'd forgotten something, and hurried into the house. She took the letter with her.

A moment later Martin went inside and poured a glass of iced tea. "Honey," he said. "Becca? Where are you?"

"In here," she called from the bathroom.

"What are you doing?"

"Oh, Martin. Honestly."

He stood outside the door. "Are you all right?"

"Of course I'm all right."

"You're going to the bathroom?"

"Martin."

"OK, I'm sorry." He stepped back from the door. "Do you have the letter in there with you?"

He heard the flutter of the toilet-paper spindle, then a flush, then water running in the sink.

She opened the door and stepped toward him, smiling. She looped her arms around his neck. "How's my little boy," she said. Her smile reminded him of one time after a party, when she had been drunk.

"Fine," he said.

She ran a hand down over his belly, and then lower. "And how's my other little boy?"

"He's fine too."

She took his hand. "Let's go to bed," she said.

"What did you do with the letter?"

"It was junk. I threw it out."

"What was it?"

"I told you, it was nothing."

"Who was it from?"

"No one."

They were in the bedroom now. This side of the house got less breeze, and the air was stale. The bed covers lay tousled and unmade, and sections of the Sunday paper were strewn about on the floor. The television remote control sat on top of Martin's pillow.

"So no one wrote you a letter about nothing."

"That's right." She took off her shorts and top, then pressed close against him. He was always startled by how white her skin was. While they were kissing she reached behind and unhooked her bra, then slid off her underpants. She had gained weight in her legs and hips, and with her clothes off this was more noticeable. "Start the fan," she whispered. "It's muggy."

She began to kiss his neck, then his chest. When she moved to her knees he said, "Wait."

She looked up. "What is it, love?"

"I want to talk about this."

She opened his fly anyway, and started.

"Rebecca," he said. "Becca."

But then they were in bed, and then they were asleep.

He woke in the dark and lay listening to the hum of the fan. The air was cooler now and he wondered if it had rained while they were sleeping. Earlier in the evening, dark-bottomed clouds had gathered overhead.

Rebecca lay on her side, facing him. He said her name, lightly, then a little louder. She didn't open her eyes.

He slipped out of bed and padded over to her clothes, which lay in a pile on the floor. He searched through her pockets for the letter. It wasn't there.

He went to the bathroom, locked the door, and searched the

drawers. He looked in the medicine cabinet behind the mirror, and in the musty-smelling space under the sink where Rebecca kept her tampons and the toilet plunger and the cans of Ajax and tile cleaner. He removed the lid of the toilet tank and peered inside—then realized he was being silly.

Once, a few months before, he'd heard Rebecca in the bedroom, talking on the phone. He heard her say, "OK, Tuesday," and when he opened the door she said, "Right then, OK, goodbye then," and hung up quickly. And so on Tuesday evening he followed her when she left work. He stayed a few cars back, watching the roof of her blue Corolla. His stomach felt weak. When she pulled into the center lane and put on her left turn signal at the entrance to the Holiday Inn, his hands began to tremble. He got into the center lane behind her; but then suddenly he became afraid that she might see him and so he pulled back out into traffic and sped past her. In his rearview mirror he saw her drive across the oncoming traffic and start up the driveway into the motel parking lot.

He sat down on the couch and tried to think where she might have put the letter. He was naked. By habit, he reached for the big glass ashtray and pulled it toward him. Then he remembered that he'd stopped smoking. It had been less than a month, but already he hardly ever missed the cigarettes.

He looked through the trash bin in the kitchen. There, where he had thrown it, was the postcard with the picture of the lost boy. He tried to imagine the boy's parents. They are about my age, he thought. Good people: they go to church, they like to barbecue on Friday nights, and in their minds their boy is still alive. He looked out into the still, silent backyards of his neighborhood. In any one of those places, he thought, there was anguish enough for all of them.

In the trash bin he found the remains of a salad and a soggy coffee filter. Then, as he stood up, he found the letter, wedged between two cookbooks. He slid the envelope out. It had not been opened. He held it up to the window, as if the dim light slanting in from the yard might let him make out the words inside.

Driving home from the Holiday Inn that night he had let himself imagine the things that were taking place in that motel room, and as he did this his anger built. But then, as he turned into the driveway of his empty ranch house and the engine of his little car coughed and sputtered and at last fell silent, his anger gave way to shame. Why had he turned away? Why couldn't he confront her? Why, all his life, had he been afraid of people? For a moment he considered driving back to the Holiday Inn and creating a scene; but instead he went inside, ate some Japanese soup, and went to bed with a book. He had done the right thing: because to have seen Tyler in the flesh, to have heard his voice, would have made him real in a way that so far he was not. For now he was a bad dream, an abstraction, a concept—he might not exist at all. And even if he did exist, he might have any number of flaws. He could be short, fat, ugly, stupid, vain, arrogant. Thinking this way, Martin began to pity Rebecca for being drawn to such a man. He imagined her coming out of the motel room and standing alone in the parking lot: a woman slipping toward middle age, silhouetted against a Holiday Inn sign and a blazing highway, where cars poured past her as pitilessly as life itself. He shut his eyes and was overcome by a tremendous sadness. When Rebecca got home he pretended to be asleep.

He went to the bedroom and dressed, then went out for a walk. The air was cool. He had the letter in his pocket, but he tried not to think about it.

He walked and walked, past the quiet houses of his neighbors, whom he envied for being able to sleep, and down the hill, across the railroad tracks, all the way downtown. The whole time he fingered the letter in his pocket. His mind rushed with possibilities: he could open the letter; he could wake Rebecca, shine a flashlight in her eyes, and make her read it in front of him; he could put it back and leave well enough alone. The last was the best, probably, but it was the one he was least likely to choose.

At the Store 24 he bought a package of Winston Lights. He lit the first one before he was out of the store, and by the time he got to Haffner's garage on Union Street he was so dizzy that he had to stop. He took the letter from his pocket, but just as he was about to open it a car drove past and caught him in the swath of its headlights. He stuffed the envelope back into his pocket, feeling as if he'd been caught committing a crime.

He walked down Union Street, past the common, where hard-looking Spanish men were gathered in clusters, smoking cigarettes. Deeper into the park he caught glimpses of prostitutes strolling on the pathways. With Susan, and with all the other women, there was this time before the end when he knew the end was coming but he didn't know when it would hit him. It was normal to turn to whores then, but that was the wrong thing to do. The thing to do was just relax and let the bad news happen.

With any luck, a new woman appeared before the old one went away. He'd met Rebecca just as Susan had begun to end things with him; it was like one wave rolling into shore while the last one washed out. She had studied in Moscow, and skied in the Alps; her British accent made the back of his neck tingle. She had rowed in college, and during the early days of their relationship he often imagined her out on the water: face set in concentration, body moving like a lever. Here, he thought, was a woman he could depend on.

He turned up Newbury Street. The air smelled like clean laundry, like sheets fresh out of the wash, and for a moment he was relieved of the sorrow of being a man moving into middle age alone, without a wife and family. But then in a bus shelter by the Napoli bakery a boy and girl were kissing, and when he stopped to watch them he felt tears in his eyes. He turned and hurried away. What was wrong with the world, he thought, when the sight of some common, ordinary thing, some lovely thing, was enough to break your heart? He lit another cigarette.

At home Rebecca was sitting on the couch, naked.

"You're up," he said.

Her hair was flattened on one side, and her face seemed to sag. She looked like someone he might have interviewed— someone whose son had been killed in a car accident, someone whose home had been destroyed by a fire.

"I went for a walk," he said.

She held out her hand and said, "May I have it, please."

He took the letter from his pocket and handed it to her. "I haven't opened it," he said.

She tapped its corner on the coffee table. He sat down in the armchair.

"I don't need to read it," she said. "I know what he wants. He wants to start up again."

He admired how well she could discuss the edges of a subject and leave out the center. He believed this was an English trait. His hands trembled. "I think I'll have a cigarette," he said. He pulled the ashtray toward him.

She stood up. He was afraid that someone walking by might see her through the bay window. But nobody was out walking at this hour, not in their neighborhood. Her breasts lay flat against her body, like half-melted snow figures.

"I don't know why," she said, "But I can't get past him."

So there it was. She crossed her arms beneath her breasts. The letter hung from her hand.

"I want to," she said, "but I can't."

"Well, don't say you don't know why. You do know why."

"You don't have to get angry."

"I'm not angry."

"That big American temper. You're all like that. There's a problem, so let's fight about it. Well I don't want to fight."

"Neither do I."

"Right, let's duke it out. Let's break something." She picked up the glass ashtray as if she might throw it against the wall. Then she put it down.

"Becca," he said, "this is ridiculous."

"I wish you wouldn't call me that."

"What should I call you?" He looked at her big, dimpled hips.

"I could think of some things."

"I'm sure you could." She slumped back onto the couch. "Martin, let's stop. I hate this. Here." She slid the letter across the table to him. "Throw this out. I don't want to read it."

He picked up the envelope. Part of him wanted very much to open the letter and read each sentence out loud, slowly. He ran his finger along the edge of the envelope.

"I want to know what you're going to do," he said. "I at least have a right to know that."

"Please," she said. "Get rid of it."

"But I at least have a right—"

"Martin, I don't know what I'm going to do."

He went to the kitchen and put the letter into the trash. It fell beside the postcard with the picture of the lost boy.

"No," she said. "Take it outside. Please."

He choked off the plastic bag and carried it out to the sidewalk with the others. He imagined Tyler and the lost boy being carted off to the dump, as if that could be the end of them. Halfway up the driveway he stopped and thought: to hell with her feelings. He was sick of looking the other way, of avoiding confrontation and pretending to be asleep. He'd had his heart ripped out and fed to him, and right or not he was going to open that letter right in her face—he'd read it out loud at the top of his lungs, and to hell with being humiliated. He was beyond humiliation. He walked back to the curb. His heart pounded up into his throat. He opened the trash bag, took out the envelope, ripped it open, and held the letter up under the light. He read:

Dear Becca,

Good news & bad news. Good news is Marie & I are finally tying the knot. Bad news is that you & I have got to stop talking. Radio silence. Even letters. She gets angry, etc., no need to tell you. Wish I could say for how long, but I can't. Maybe forever.

You know I'll think of you, & I can't say I won't have fond memories. Wish you the best, & for Martin too. Bet he's not so bad. Marry him?

Again, sorry. All best wishes—Tyler.

He read the closing line again, trying to imagine the kind of man who would end this sort of letter that way. After all these years, that was the best he could do? His hands shook as he put the letter back into the trash and tied off the bag.

He was angry and happy and sad and relieved; all these feelings flew and tangled in his heart like leaves in the wind. He stood still for a moment. Life, it seemed, had surprised him with good news; however it was a bitter trick to get what you wanted but to get it by default. The street lamps cast pale light into the leaves of the elm trees. He threw his cigarettes into the trash.

Inside, he undressed and got into bed beside Rebecca. He felt alert and electric; his skin bristled. He could not be still. For a long time they were silent. He began to think she was asleep. Then she turned on her side and said, "Martin, I want to be Buddhist about this."

He opened his eyes. His heart was racing. "You mean shave our heads, the whole thing?"

"I mean the philosophy," she said.

She said she wanted there to be no past, no future—just the present. She wanted to live for the moment. "Do you understand what I'm saying? I'm saying that I can't make you any promises."

"I understand," he said.

But soon, he knew, she would blunder into Tyler's bad news, and then a change would occur. One day he would come home and she would have bought him a necktie, or she'd want to plan a picnic, and her heart, which for so long had stood half-closed to him, would now be wide and inviting. She would never say what had happened, and he would not ask.

He would not ask because he would not care; because by then he would no longer love her. Already, in just these few minutes, he had begun to despise her. Part of him wanted to jump up and storm out to the car and leave and never look back. His blood crashed and roared through his veins; he felt as if he might scream. How could you accept a life like this? Still, he would accept Rebecca. He was too old to start over again. He felt as if he'd been robbed or cheated—as if God were some oily con man who had just got the better of him and now was laughing up His sleeve. All at once the galling transaction that was his life—small moments of joy stained by the awful price he would pay for them—became apparent to him. He coughed, then cleared his throat.

Rebecca turned onto one side, and then the other. She lay face down, then rolled onto her back. "Oh, damn, I can't sleep," she said finally.

For a moment they lay still. A breeze ruffled the curtains. She turned her head toward him and said, "Martin, I have a confession to make."

He rolled onto his side and gazed at her: the sad, earnest, foolish face; the weak chin; the pale thin neck, which only with effort could he keep his hands from grasping. His fingers clutched at a roll of the bed sheet, squeezing and releasing it.

"I don't want to hear it," he said.

"It's driving me mad."

"No," he said. "Not now."

In a few minutes her head fell to the side and she began to snore lightly into her pillow. The sky outside became gray, then pink. The yard seethed with insects. As tired as he was, he didn't think he would be able to sleep.

The Clear Blue

THEY DREW ME into their scheme with a birthday present. On July 16, my eighteenth birthday, I came home from a yard job in Edmunds to find the kitchen decorated with streamers and balloons. Before I could realize what was happening, my mother and Grace and Tom leapt out from the back hall and sang "Happy Birthday." They cooked lobsters and steamers, and the ocean smell reminded me of the summers when my father still lived with us. After dinner I went to my room.

"Strange to see you moping on your birthday," Grace said, after she'd come upstairs and barged into my room without knocking. Grace was my mother's new best friend. They'd met in Hillcrest Hospital, where my mother had spent the month of June, doing what she called "rehabilitating."

I said I didn't think it was unusual for me to be moping; in fact sadness seemed to be the emotion best suited to the occasion of leaving your childhood behind, I said, and anyway this was beside the point because I could only feel the way I felt, which was sad, and trying to feel another way would only make me feel sadder. "So there's nothing I can do about it," I said.

While I was speaking she had begun to laugh, as if I were telling a joke, and she did not stop laughing until I stopped talking. Then she caught her breath and said, "Bryan, you think too much."

I had a mother who drank and dried out in hospitals, a father and brother who lived three thousand miles away; I was eighteen years old, mowing lawns for a living—I had to bid against junior high school kids; it was ridiculous—and I didn't have a scratch of an idea of what to do with my life. "Do you blame me?" I said.

She sat down on the bed. She was a heavy woman, and the mattress sagged beneath her weight so that I tilted toward her. She put her arm around my shoulders. "You know what you need?"

"Umm . . . to be left alone?"

She frowned. "No. What you need is to get the shit scared out of you."

Our school psychologist liked to use the word *fuck* during our sessions—a technique that I supposed was designed to jar me out of my black moods. Instead he just sounded foolish.

I told her, no offense, but growing up with my mother had given me plenty of chances to get the *shit* scared out of me. I asked her if she ever wondered why none of our crystal sets was complete. She said she knew all about crystal sets.

"So tell me," she said. "Have you ever jumped out of an airplane?"

Until then I still hadn't decided whether to hate Grace. But now I was certain.

"Hundreds of times," I said.

She handed me a book of Hemingway short stories and an envelope. "Open it," she said.

Inside was a gift certificate from Lawton Falls Airport for skydiving lessons. The card had a drawing of a man soaring with his arms and legs out, like a flying squirrel.

"Be honest," I said. "You want me dead, right?"

"Your mom and I are going, too."

I would sooner have believed almost anything about my mother than that she was going to jump out of an airplane. I told Grace that they had been too generous, that a gift certificate at Record Town would have been plenty. I told her she should use my skydiving certificate for herself.

"No dice," she said. "We're making the big leap, and you're coming with us. And read that Hemingway. Now that was a guy who understood about courage."

One night when we were young David and I huddled in the front hall and watched our mother hurl plates across the kitchen at our father, who ducked and let them explode against the wall like clay pigeons in a skeet range. When she was out of plates she began to throw glasses which to my surprise did not burst as cleanly or completely as the plates but fell into the pile at my father's feet in big, jagged chunks.

The point of this is that later, when her drinking became worse and her aim—inexplicably—got better, I understood why David and my father moved away. What I didn't understand was why people like Grace and my mother kept going, after all they'd been through.

"Why does grass grow?" my mother said. "I don't know." She had stopped coloring her hair when she went into the hospital, and now it was shot through with gray. "Why did you stay here instead of going to California?" she said.

I shrugged. "I don't know."

"You see?" She smiled, as if she'd made a point. Then she became serious. She said, "I know why you stayed."

"Tell me," I said.

She waved her hands, the way she did when she was embarrassed. "Someday you'll know," she said.

She and Grace were schoolteachers, and that summer they

both taught at the J. G. Whittier Middle School in North Edmunds. Like my mother, Grace was divorced and living on a meager settlement. They'd both spent plenty of time in hospitals, and sometimes at night they'd sit out on our porch and trade hospital war stories: men who shouted and cried all night, women who tore the hair from their scalps.

They went to AA meetings seven nights a week, and I think they spent as much time flirting with men as they did listening to the stories, because within two weeks Grace had found Tom and bulldozed him into becoming her boyfriend. And it was at another AA meeting that they had met the man who would be our skydiving jump coach.

"His name is Hal," my mother said. "Captain Hal Martin."

We were at the kitchen table, eating my birthday cake. Grace had dragged me downstairs with my Hemingway book and my skydiving certificate.

"He's a real character," Tom said. "You'll love him."

"Wait a minute," I said. "Our leader is, well—he's one of you?"

Grace scowled. "Don't worry, he won't be driving the plane."

"Will he be packing the chutes?"

Tom laughed, but Grace shot him a look and he quietly began eating his cake again. Tom ran a funeral home; he was a soft-spoken little man who had begun drinking after his mother died. He always wore a tan golf jacket, no matter how hot it was, and he had soft, fleshy hands that were as white as talcum powder.

"And what about you," I asked my mother. "You're really going?"

"Of course she's going," Grace said.

"Of course I'm going," she said.

I watched her lift her cup of coffee to her lips. There'd been a time when she couldn't hold a cup steady enough to drink from it. I waited for her to wink and clue me in on the joke. She looked up. "What?" she said. "You're afraid?"

"Of jumping out of a plane at twenty thousand feet? All right, yes, I'm afraid—OK?"

"It's not twenty thousand feet."

"It's three thousand," Grace said.

"Oh, well, that's different. Three thousand feet."

"It's not like you just go up there and jump out. You get lessons. You know what you're doing."

I pointed out that two lessons at the Lawton Falls Airport, and from Captain Hal, no less, were hardly enough to make me feel safe about taking my life in my hands.

"You know," Grace said, "it's a shame, but men just don't have balls anymore."

"Excuse me?" I said.

My mother smiled and looked down at the table.

"Yes, what's this?" Tom said, trying to be indignant.

"Oh, for Christ's sake, you've heard of balls before," Grace said. "You might've seen a pair, if you've looked down lately."

He put down his fork and stopped eating.

"You see what I mean?" she said. "Ann, these guys are scared to death of us. We use their language, we say a *swear* word"—she smiled and poked Tom in the side, but he didn't smile—"and it scares the *shit* out of them. They can't even ask us out anymore. They're all sensitive and afraid of getting hurt. Or they're afraid of commitment. Jesus H. Christ! And the ones who do somehow manage to get themselves married—what do they do but walk out on their wives!"

"Amen," my mother said.

"I mean," Grace said, "what the hell is going on here? What is everyone so goddamn afraid of?"

She stopped then, taken aback by Tom's gloomy expression and perhaps by the sense of how loud her voice had become.

Tom pushed his cake around on his plate. "You know damn well what we're afraid of," he said.

From the Duggans' yard came the throaty sound of a lawnmower: it was Tommy Minihan, the fourteen-year-old who had underbid me, using his father's self-propelled Toro. But other than that the evening was quiet. The daylight had faded, and dusk was settling over the neighborhood.

The next day we took my mother's new Nissan Stanza—a car whose smallness seemed to point out our reduced circumstances—and drove to North Conway to take a gondola ride. This was Grace's idea. She said it was a dry run for the skydive. "We need a taste of danger," she said, "before the full meal."

She sought out anything steep or fast; roller coasters and motorcycles were high on her list. Her theory was that weakness in spirit was what led people to drink, and that facing fear was a way to overcome weakness in spirit. My take was that being in life-threatening situations simply kept her so flat-out, white-knuckled scared that she couldn't think of drinking; or maybe the feeling of being scared was just a substitute for the feeling of being drunk.

Either way it didn't matter to me on that gondola. As we lurched up over the cliffs and outcroppings, with the wind knocking us around, I sat on the edge of the bench and stared down at my feet, concentrating on the patterns in the corrugated metal floor. Sweat beaded up between my shoulder blades. I ignored Grace's chatter about how far you could see from up here, and tried not to think about the two small bolts and the even smaller cotter pins by which our car was attached to the cable.

"Just think of that old Francis Macomber," Grace said. "He'd be right up here at the window."

"Why don't you climb out and ride on the roof?" I said.

After the gondola ride we drove into town and Grace and my mother ran through the stores in the strip malls like Marines taking a village, sifting through clothing racks and calling to each other, while Tom and I stood nearby, trying to make small talk. Tom, to his credit, did not try to play father to me; and ironically there was something about his timidity that inspired me—the idea being, I suppose, that if he could make his way in the world, then so could I.

Later, at lunch, trouble struck. For no apparent reason, my mother began to cry.

The waitress headed toward our table. I stood up and said we should go outside.

"No, I'm OK," my mother said. "I'm OK." But then she began to cry again.

In the car she cried even harder, until finally she was shaking. Grace got in back and held her, but she couldn't calm her down. I sat in front with Tom, who kept wondering out loud whether he should start the car and head home, or wait another minute.

"Ann," Grace said. "Annie. It's all right."

"It's not all right. It's all shit, is what it is."

Grace rubbed her head. "Everything's all right. We're all here. It's all right."

"It's not all right."

"Ann, take it easy. Relax."

"I want a drink, OK? I looked at that menu . . . I didn't think I did, I mean I thought I was past it, but I'm not. I'm right where I began."

"That's all right too."

"It's not all right."

Grace was working to stay calm. She looked at me. "This is good," she said. "Really. It's a good sign. It means she's about to break through."

"Yes," Tom said. "I've heard of this."

But clearly this was a setback. All those nights out on the screened porch, chuckling about the world as if finally she was safe from it, had lulled my mother into forgetting that the problem was not the world—it was herself. Now, in a strip mall parking lot in North Conway, New Hampshire, she was having a good look into her rusty, rickety soul, and it was not a pleasant sight. We rode home in silence. Tom drove with both hands on the wheel.

As we passed by Mount Chocorua and then headed across the Kancamagus Highway, with Tom staring at the road as if he were driving on the edge of a cliff, my old fears came back at me. Life could blind-side you in an instant: a car could swerve into you; an aneurism could burst in your head; a nuclear flash, quick as the snap of a finger, could turn these White Mountains into New England's own Grand Canyon.

That evening we sat on the porch again. My mother talked gloomily about coloring her hair. Grace talked about jump position and tandem jump techniques, but when none of us responded she finally gave up.

Captain Hal Martin met us at the snack bar at the airport. He was a tall thin man with a close-cropped military haircut and a scraggly mustache. He shook our hands and took us to his office, which was down the hall from the snack bar. The office had fake wood paneling on the walls and a suspended ceiling that was missing a tile in the corner. On the walls were photographs of Captain Hal with various people in jump suits, holding helmets under their arms. Captain Hal's desk was covered with stacks of paper and discarded Styrofoam coffee cups.

"So, my friends," he said when we'd settled into plastic chairs. "You want to jump out of a plane—is that right?"

"That's right," Grace said, while the rest of us nodded.

He leaned over his desk. "What are you—crazy?"

He howled with laughter, and we said yes, we were crazy, and we laughed uneasily and shifted in our seats. He looked at me, and then at Tom and Grace. Then he looked at my mother and his milky eyes grew wide and he held his gaze on her just long enough to make me feel uneasy.

"Now, you *do* want parachutes—is that right? You don't want to just fall."

My mother blushed.

"That's right," Grace said. "We want the parachutes."

Right then I knew that I hated Captain Hal, and that jumping from a plane was going to be a relief after the ordeal of his lessons. We spent an hour enduring his stale jokes and trying to pay attention to his instructions on how to steer the chute by pulling on the cords and kicking with your legs, and how to roll to the side when you landed.

"The most important thing is your diving posture. Here," he said to my mother. "Ann, stand up and face the wall."

My mother was small—her head came about even with Captain Hal's chest—and the sight of them standing together made me uncomfortable. He stood behind her, grinning. "Now the rest of you pay attention," he said, "because this posture is crucial." He put his hands on my mother's hips, as if they were going to do the bunny hop. "OK. Now, Ann, put your hands out and up. That's it. Out and up. A ninety-degree angle from your shoulders. Good. Palms open."

He turned to us. "You see?"

We nodded. My mother looked like someone being held at gunpoint.

"Now open up your stance," he said.

"What?"

"Move your feet apart. A little more. Shoulder width." He placed his foot between her legs and knocked her feet apart. "That's it. Now arch your back and bend your knees."

Her rear end stuck out toward him. I imagined him telling this story to his buddies in the airport cocktail lounge later that afternoon.

"A little more," he said. She giggled. He squeezed her waist. "Don't worry, Ann, I've got you."

She bent further, until her rear end was almost touching the front of his pants. She looked as if she were about to soar out the window like Wonder Woman. Captain Hal turned to us. "OK, so remember this," he said. "Arms up and out, feet apart, knees bent. Got it?"

"Etched in stone," Grace said.

He released his grip on my mother's waist and stood back. She glanced over her shoulder with a disappointed look in her eyes. "Are we done?" she said. "That's it?"

I slid her chair forward. "Mom, sit down," I said.

There had been few men in my mother's life since my father, and none had ever become serious. She said she kept them at a distance for my sake. "It's confusing to a boy," she said. But this was a lie: she was lonely and desperate and wanted more than anything to have a boyfriend. That, in fact, was what kept them away.

So I was surprised to answer the doorbell a few nights after our skydiving lesson to find Captain Hal standing on our front steps with a bouquet of flowers in his hand. We stood facing each other for a moment; I fought the urge to close the door in his face.

"Oh, Hal, you're early," my mother said from behind me. She squeezed my shoulder so hard that it hurt, and moved me away from the door.

He handed her the flowers. "They're jonquils," he said.

"Well, I'll be," she said.

She held the bouquet in both hands and admired it as if she'd never seen flowers before. When she went back upstairs to finish getting ready, Captain Hal sat on the couch and I sat in the armchair, glowering at the television.

"We're going to the Topsfield Fair," he said.

I imagined him winning a big stuffed bear for her, or feeding her cotton candy, or standing behind her at the pellet-gun booth with his arms around her, teaching her how to shoot—he was the kind of man who would actually do that. Maybe he would take her to a bar; he was probably the kind of man who would do that, too.

"Great," I said, then pretended to be interested in the game show.

After they left I opened the Hemingway book and read the story about Francis Macomber again. I did not have a code to live by, and I needed one. But what would mine be? Love your neighbor as yourself? Always tell the truth? I had no idea. I finished the story and started another, but then I got bored and went to bed.

They returned late. I lay listening to Captain Hal's Cadillac engine idling in our driveway for a long time, trying not to imagine the embarrassing, awkward things that were probably taking place in that car. Finally I heard my mother's voice, the car door shutting, and the click of her shoes on the front walk. Captain Hal drove off. I listened, expecting to hear the sounds of backsliding: her bumping into a chair, scattering the pens off the top of the cutting block, the clink of ice cubes in a glass. But instead there was the soft padding of her bare feet on the kitchen floor, the tiny groan of each stair as she moved smoothly up to her room, and the splash of water in the bathroom sink.

Saturday morning I found myself sitting Indian style in the hold of a Cessna airplane three thousand feet above the ground, with two middle-aged schoolteachers and a man who embalmed dead bodies. I was startled—literally amazed—to find myself there; it was as if all the events that had led to that moment had taken place in a dream, while I was sleeping. And now I was awake—perilously, scalp-tinglingly awake. More awake, in fact, than I cared to be.

In our space suits and helmets we were tight-faced and solemn. Even Grace was silent. The three of them held hands and closed their eyes and prayed; I was reminded of the time my mother went on a weekend prayer retreat where she'd had to stay in a room all day and couldn't even leave to use the bathroom. Now they were praying that this display of courage would sandblast their souls and send them back into the world sober, free of desire. My goal was to land without breaking my legs.

Captain Hal stood near the cockpit, braced against the frame tubes that ran the length of the plane. He grinned and said something that got lost in the drone of the engines. My mother smiled and nodded anyway, as if she had heard him. He smiled back at her. I was certain that behind his mirrored sunglasses he was leering at her.

During our second lesson he had found a new way to get his paws on her, by using her to demonstrate how to run the harness straps of the parachute up between the thighs and across the buttocks.

The Lawton Falls we saw from the sky might have been a different city altogether. There were more trees than I'd realized, and from this height the blemishes were erased, so that beneath us was a quilt of green baseball fields, red brick mills, white cemeteries, and shiny silver used car lots. I could make out Beshara's restaurant and the Napoli bakery and Tom's funeral home and the Lawton Falls High football stadium. The canals spread off from the river and ran parallel to each other like the tines of a fork, glinting in the sun.

The pilot slowed the engine and we could hear what Captain Hal was saying: Stand up, he told us, check your static lines, hold the rail in the roof of the plane and get ready. Not a minute later, timid Tom Doyle, lionized by his love for a woman, stepped out onto the platform and hurled himself into the sky, and in those awful seconds before his chute opened I am certain he did not care whether he lived or died. Grace followed. My mother held my hand while we watched Grace plummet; when her chute burst open with a pop my mother squeezed my hand, then let go and stepped out onto the jump spot.

I took her arm. "Any last words?"

She peered at me through her goggles. "Don't forget to water the plants," she shouted. Then she smiled and dove away. The sight of your mother dressed like a commando and hurtling toward the earth is an extraordinary one. I stepped out onto the narrow platform, holding tight against the current beneath the wing, and watched as her chute streamed out, bloomed, and caught the air. I looked at Captain Hal. He smiled and gave me the thumbs-up sign. "Head up," he yelled, "and let me see a good strong arch."

I nodded. I fought the urge to look down.

"Go," he said.

I hesitated; and then I looked down. And all at once I realized where I was: clinging to the wing strut of an airplane like a circus stuntman. I froze.

"Go," he shouted again.

I reached for the door. "I'm coming back inside," I said.

Then Captain Hal did something that I am sure was extraordinary, even for him: hanging like a chimp from the frame, he swung his legs out, pressed a boot into my ribs, and kicked me out into the wild blue yonder. By instinct I sprang into jump position—back arched, neck bent—and hurtled toward the earth.

For ten seconds I dropped, arms and legs out, like a spider on a string, and not until the line paid out and the chute caught open and the straps snugged tight around my legs did I realize what had happened. By then I was glad to have been pushed, because it was not at all frightening; the wonder overshadowed the fear. Soaring above my hometown, I realized my life could go in any of a thousand directions. The world beckoned, and for the first time, the idea of making my way into it did not seem frightening. I landed in a fallow field behind the airstrip, wide of the target.

Captain Hal touched down in the center of the target. He did not fall and roll, but simply bent his legs, then straightened up and began to reel in his chute. He walked over to where we were standing, took my mother in his arms, and kissed her.

"Hell of a jump," he said. He winked at me over her shoulder. "Hell of a first jump."

An hour later we were pulling into a Friendly's for lunch when Tom said, "I will never be scared again." He rapped his hand on the dashboard. "I mean, by God, I will never again be scared. Of anything."

"All right already," Grace said. "Jesus Christ."

Grace had goofed her landing and sprained her ankle. Tom stopped laughing and steered into a parking space.

"I will never drink again," my mother said in a soft voice.

Grace turned around in her seat. "Come again?"

"I'm not making a promise. I'm just stating a fact." She stared down at her hands. "Right now I know that I will never taste alcohol again. I just know it."

She lay her face against my chest and began to cry. Then she began to laugh, too, and she heaved with laughter and crying. It was as if all the poison from all those years was draining from her. "Mom," I said. "Mom, it's over now. It's over."

"Yes," Hal said. "It's over."

He put his hand on her arm, and she turned away from me then and fell against him.

That night Tom bought a white sheet cake from the Napoli bakery. The cake had the image of a parachutist drawn with red frosting on the top. We had ice cream with the cake, and iced coffee. Hal made a toast to the future.

Later, my mother called me out to the yard. The air was cool and scented with the odor of dogwood blossoms. She wore a green summer dress and a pair of white canvas boat shoes. Her eyes were wide and clear, and although her hair was gray she was still young and still pretty. We sat on the slope where one summer she had tried to make a Japanese rock garden.

"I have something to tell you," she said. "I want you to take it the right way."

There was no breeze; I listened to the cars out on the interstate. I imagined the great moving mass of them, the road glowing like a river of light.

"Hal and I are going to get serious," she said. "We're going to make a life with each other."

"Oh," I said.

She smiled and said, "I'm happier than I've ever been. I feel like a girl again."

I lay back and looked at the stars and the thin clouds moving quickly overhead.

"I'm a pretty good judge of people," she said, "and I think he's a decent man. Don't you think he's a decent man?"

For years I had prayed that she would get her life together;

now she had and it seemed like the worst thing that ever happened. She was going to marry a man who had pushed me from an airplane.

"I'm sure he's decent," I said.

"He wants to help you, too," she said. "With college, or whatever."

"What do you mean by whatever?" I said.

She shrugged and looked away. I knew what she meant.

I rose up and stood before her with my hands by my side, suddenly feeling big and clumsy, like somebody blocking an aisle in a supermarket. She stood up too. I felt ashamed and silly. I started to turn away, but she took my arm.

"Wait," she said.

She took my face in her hands, pulled me toward her, and kissed me on the mouth. She stepped back, gave me a girlish, embarrassed smile, and turned and walked toward the house. It occurred to me then that life became more confusing, not less, as you got older; that each solution created a new problem; and that trouble didn't go away but just moved from person to person. When I opened my eyes she was in the deep shade near the porch, nearly invisible, reaching for the screen door. I hurried across the darkened yard after her.

The Birthday Cake

THE AIR WAS COLD and the daylight was draining from the sky. The street smelled of rotten fruit left in the carts and although this was a sour smell it was not altogether unpleasant. Lucia was accustomed to this odor, and because it reminded her of the feast days when she was a girl she enjoyed it, the way she imagined people on farms enjoyed the smell of manure.

It was past six and the shops on Newbury Street were closed, but she knew that Lorenzo would stay open for her. She did not hurry: she was an old woman, and age had spoiled her legs. They were thick now, and water heavy, and when she walked her hips grew sore from the effort of moving them.

She stopped by a bench, wanting to sit but knowing that to stoop and then to rise would be more difficult than simply to lean against the backrest. She waited for her breathing to slow, then walked the last block to the bakery. Lorenzo would be there. He would wait. Hadn't she come to the bakery every Saturday since the war? And hadn't she bought the same white cake with chocolate frosting, Nico's favorite?

"Buona sera, Signora Ronsavelli," he said as the chime clanged and the heavy glass door closed behind her. "You had me concerned."

Lorenzo Napoli was too young to be so worried all the time. She wondered about him. She did not trust him the way she had trusted his father.

Standing before the pastry case was Maria Mendez, the little Puerto Rican girl who worked at the laundry. "Este es la señora," Lorenzo said to her. They were everywhere now, these Puerto Ricans, all over the neighborhood with their loud cars and shouting children and men drinking beer on the sidewalk. Now the rents were increasing and the real estate people wanted the Italians to move to nursing homes. Even Father D'Agostino was helping them. "Lucia," the priest had told her, "you'd have company there."

This Maria from the laundry had a child but no husband. She smiled at Lucia, then peered down into the glass case.

"Miss Mendez needs to ask you a favor," the baker said.

Lucia removed her leather gloves and put them into her purse. "A favor?"

"My little girl," Maria said. "Today is her birthday. She's seven years old today."

"You must know little Teresa," Lorenzo said.

"Yes," Lucia said. She had indeed seen the child, out with her friends tearing up the vegetable gardens in the backyards.

"And I was so busy today at the laundry, so busy, all day long there was a line, and I couldn't get out to buy her a birthday cake."

"Yes." Lucia remembered that it had taken her two days to fix the stakes for her tomato plants.

"Let me explain," Lorenzo said. "Miss Mendez needs a cake, and I have none left, except yours. I told her that you were my best customer, and of course we'd have to wait and ask you."

"All the other bakeries are closed," Maria said. "It's my little girl's birthday."

Lucia's hands began to shake. She remembered what the

doctor had said about getting angry; but this was too much. "Every week I buy my cake. For how many years? And now this *muli* comes in and you just give it away?"

"Lucy." Lorenzo held out his hands like a little boy. "Don't get angry. Please, Lucy."

"No. Not Lucy." She tapped her chest with her finger. "Lucia."

"Lucy, please," he said.

"No 'Please, Lucy.' No parlare Inglese. Italiano."

"I could give you some sugar cookies," he said. "Or some cannolis. I just made them. They're beautiful."

"Once a week I come here and I buy Nico's cake."

Lorenzo tipped his head to the side. He seemed to be about to say something, but then he stopped. He waited another moment.

"Lucia, think of the poor little girl," he said. "It's her birthday."

"Then bake her a cake. You do the favor, if you like her so much."

"Lucia, there's no time." The party was going to begin in a few minutes, he said. Besides, he had already cleaned his equipment and put away his flour and eggs and sugar.

"Lucia," he said, "it's the right thing. Ask yourself, what would Nico do? Or my father?"

"I know what they wouldn't do. They wouldn't forget who their people were. They wouldn't start speaking Spanish for the *mulis.*"

She stared at him until he looked away. Outside, the wind had lifted a newspaper from the sidewalk and was pressing the leaves against the front window of the bakery. From somewhere on Common Street came the sound of a car's engine racing. She thought of Nico, how when he lay sick in bed during his last days she had gone outside and asked the children not to make noise and they'd laughed and told her to go on back inside, crazy old lady.

Without looking up, he spoke in a voice that was almost a whisper. "Lucia," he said, "it's just this once."

"No," she said. "No. I want my cake."

Maria began to cry. "Dios mio," she said. "My little girl."

Lorenzo leaned on his hands. "I'm sorry, Miss Mendez."

Maria turned to her. She was sobbing. "It's my daughter's birthday," she said. "How will she forgive me? Don't you have children?"

"I have three children," Lucia said. "And I never forgot their birthdays. I never had to rush out at the last minute."

"I was working," Maria said. "I'm all by myself with Teresa. I have to raise her alone."

"And whose fault is that?" Lucia waved at Lorenzo. "Pronto," she said. "Box up my cake."

Lorenzo eased the cake out of the display case and placed it into a white cardboard pastry box. His hands were soft and white. He drew a length of twine from the dispenser, tied off the box, then snapped his wrists and broke the string from the leader.

Lucia put on her gloves. As she turned for the door Maria took her arm. "I'll beg you," she said. "Please, I'll buy the cake from you. I'll pay you ten dollars."

Lucia pulled her arm free. "I don't want your money."

"Twenty dollars, then." She pulled a folded bill from the pocket of her dress and placed it in Lucia's hand. "Please, Mrs. Ronsavelli, take it."

Lucia tried to push the bill back into her hands, but Maria curled her fingers into fists and began to cry. "You can't do this," she said.

Lucia threw the crumpled bill to the floor and opened the door. Maria fell to her knees and picked up the bill. "You witch!" she screamed. "Puta! Whore!"

Lucia did not look back. She moved slowly down Newbury Street, being careful to avoid the spots of ice. What did that laundry girl, or even Lorenzo, understand about her? What did they know about devotion?

From the alley behind her building she heard the screaming, a terrible choked wail that rang from the street and into the alley and echoed off the walls and trash cans. She imagined Maria the laundress stumbling home to her daughter, and she imagined the red, contorted face of the little girl when her friends arrived and there was no cake.

Still, what would they know about suffering, even then? They would know nothing. The light was poor in the staircase, and she held the railing with her free hand. After each step she paused; she let the flicker of pain ease from her hips, then lifted again.

Inside the kitchen she raised the glass cover and took out last week's cake. The air that had been under the glass smelled sweet and ripe. The cake had not been touched; it might have been a clay model of the new one. As she carried it to the trash, tips of chocolate frosting broke off and scattered on the floor like shards of pottery.

She swept up the pieces, washed the smudges of frosting from the cake stand with a sponge, then opened the bakery box, removed the new cake and put it under the glass cover. It was dark outside, and in the hills around the city the lights in the windows of hundreds of houses glowed like the tiny white bulbs in the branches of a Christmas tree. She thought of her children; they were up in those hills, eating dinner with their own children—those little light-skinned boys and girls who shrank from their nana's hugs, kept their jackets on, and whispered to each other until it was time to leave. It was cold near the window; she shivered and stepped away.

She sat at the kitchen table, beneath the photos of Nico and the children. She looked at the door, wishing, as she did each time, that there might be a knock, or that it might just swing open, and one of them, just one of them, might be there.

New Math

DURING MY sixth-grade year at St. Michael School I somehow lost the ability to do math, and suddenly I, Patrick Fitzgerald—science fair winner, spelling bee champ—found myself having to be tutored. Earlier that year my mother had left us to live with a divorced orthopedic surgeon named Rudolph Freedman. This was 1968, a time when our parish was adjusting to the reforms of Vatican II, and when all the rest of the world seemed to be changing too. It was an uncertain time when things that had been solid became, for a little while, fluid; it was a time that changed each of us, and not necessarily for the better.

My math tutor was Sister Louise, our homeroom teacher. She was new to our school. She played guitar and sang "Kumbaya" at folk Masses, and when she sang she bent her notes like a pop singer. She was not much older than the high school girls we saw walking to school in the morning; in fact if she had been in their uniform, instead of her habit, she could have passed for one. Perhaps to make her look older, she wore a veil—something most of the younger nuns had given up. Her veil was not the large-brimmed, old-fashioned kind, but rather a simple length of blue cloth that attached at her hairline and fell to her shoulders, covering her head completely and focusing attention on her features: a straight, slim nose and pale blue eyes that moved slowly and seemed to rest on you as she spoke. Her skin was smooth and white, with faint freckles that were visible only when you were up close and the light reflected off the desk onto her face.

She was from Nova Scotia and she had an accent—she pronounced "th" as "t"—and her voice tended to rise on the last word of a sentence. During our sessions she sat very close to me, so close in fact that our legs pressed together and I could smell a trace of baby powder beneath her habit. She gave me Cokes from the teachers' room, and she teased me about girls.

"You and Virginia Brighton," she said once. "There's something going on, I think."

I told her I hated Virginia Brighton. "She has red hair," I said. She opened her textbook. "So you don't like red hair."

"She looks like Bozo. You know who Bozo is?"

She said yes, she knew who Bozo was. Then she smiled and said we were going to get along just fine.

David Reilly said my mother was going to be excommunicated. She would spend eternity in hell, he said. Every day he would circle me in the schoolyard, chanting, "Adultery, adultery," until finally one day I chased him down and caught him.

I pinned him down on the pavement against the chain-link fence and I leapt onto his back and tore at his uniform. We fought hockey style: he curled up his knees and rolled his head down, while I pulled his shirt over his head and punched him through it. Traffic on Andover Street backed up as people stopped to watch; two men in a delivery truck cheered me on. The rest of the class formed a circle around us. I had just drawn blood—there was a stain on his shirt where his face must have been—when a whistle split the air and everyone ran, leaving me and David Reilly alone in the yard, facing Sister Constance, the huge nun who taught Reilly's class. Behind her, like the sun hidden by the moon during an eclipse, stood Sister Louise. She was biting her bottom lip.

Constance told Sister Louise to take Reilly to the lavatory to wash up. Then she grabbed me by my hair and dragged me, like a cat, to the principal's office.

Constance was not a nun to cross. She taught social studies and she often showed us a film about the atomic bomb: we watched, again and again, the flash of light, and then the great mushroom cloud lifting itself off the floor of the desert. She accused the girls of smoking, and she told us stories about the devil. Satan, she said, sometimes took the form of a man who went to nightclubs, lured women out to his car, and murdered them. He also regularly telephoned one of the priests in our parish.

Our principal, Sister Jean Marie, was even bigger than Constance. She was in fact the biggest of the nuns—or Huns, as they were known. She'd been chosen principal because of her size, we all supposed. We called her Tanker. She wore tiny metal glasses that made her face look even bigger than it was. She had come to St. Michael School from a school in Roxbury where students carried guns and had babies in seventh grade. After meeting her at PTA my father said he believed that in a fair fight, she could take him. "And nuns never fight fair," he said.

She sat with her hands folded on her desk. Her hands were huge; each finger was the size of an Italian sausage. Why, she wanted to know, had I attacked David Reilly?

I explained that Reilly had been telling everyone that my mother was going to go to hell.

"But Patrick," she said, "that's no reason to hit him."

I said that, no offense, but it seemed like a perfectly good reason to hit him.

She let silence hang for a moment, then said, "Patrick, I know about your parents. It's been a difficult year for you, hasn't it?"

I nodded. I was thinking that maybe I should cry. My friend Jimmy D'Amato said that whenever you went to the principal's office you should begin to cry immediately. D'Amato was from a poor family, and the nuns hit him extra hard.

"You know," Tanker said, "Jesus had a hard life, too. His family was poor. And His parents were human—they fought sometimes too, you know."

"I know," I said, although I could not imagine that the Blessed Mother had ever run off with a rich doctor and left Joseph and Jesus to fend for themselves.

"Patrick," Tanker said, "what would Jesus do when the other boys picked on him?"

I let the first tear fall from my eye. "Turn the other cheek?"

She smiled. "That's right. Will you do that?"

"Yes." I began to cry. I lifted my face up and smiled through my tears, trying to look like the boy Jesus in the pictures in our catechism book.

She smiled and stood up. "Good. Now turn around and lean over the chair," she said, and lifted a pointer from behind her desk.

My mother admired the nuns. Once in fact she'd told me that she might have become a nun herself, if she hadn't met my father. And so all that day, as I dragged my sore little legs from class to class, and held myself up off the seats, I imagined her as a sister, wearing a blue habit and clunky shoes. This image gave me comfort.

For a while I had wished my mother would just come home and put everything back to normal. But I really couldn't imagine her returning. Dr. Freedman was one of the richest men in the Merrimack Valley. He owned a huge house in Edmunds. Once, on a Sunday drive, my father and I drove past Dr. Freedman's big ranch house. My mother's station wagon was in the driveway. The house had a row of smooth, perfect bushes in front. The backyard was enclosed with a gray picket fence. "Tennis court," my father whispered, as we crept past. "And a pool."

My father was a millwright at the Osgood Mill, and we lived in a three-decker on Tower Hill, the Irish neighborhood. Our life was full of cut corners, of pennies saved, but until my mother left I'd been oblivious to this. Now I was all too aware of the vulgarity of our lives. Sometimes when I walked inside and saw the old wallpaper, the yellowed window shades, the gas station glasses, and the department store dinner plates, I winced and ran to my room.

My mother had gone to junior college, and she had managed to give our life a sort of shabby dignity. At dinner she insisted that we be calm and wait until everything was served before we began to eat. Despite my father's protestations (vehement when he'd been drinking) that manners were ridiculous, given that there were just the three of us, my mother's wishes prevailed: we put our paper napkins on our laps, kept our elbows off the table, said "please" and "thank you," and contained the conversation to pleasant topics. "Manners and education," my mother told me, "are what allow us to rise above our station."

Now she had risen, and I had fallen. The calamity had cast me in an entirely new light at school: boys like D'Amato, tough kids who had transferred from public schools, now saw me as one of their own. Instead of the straight-A class president, I was the product of a broken home—hardened and streetwise.

I swore and spat; I scuffed my feet in the library and gave Virginia Brighton static electricity shocks that made her cry out. I failed tests and laughed about it.

Every time I got into trouble the nuns told me they could see a black mark on my soul. And sure enough one afternoon, when she'd come to pick me up, my mother looked down my throat and told me the nuns were right. "Yes, there's a black mark," she said. "You'll have to have it wiped off in confession."

I said we might not want to get onto the subject of black marks. We didn't speak for the rest of the afternoon.

Twice a week my mother picked me up after school and took me to a restaurant, where she sipped Manhattans and watched me eat while we both tried clumsily to have a conversation. I usually ordered something expensive, just to spite her.

The day of my beating she was due to pick me up, but she was late. Two nights a week, I thought, and she couldn't even manage that. I was lucky she remembered my name anymore.

"Look, it's no problem," Sister Louise said. "This gives us more time for math."

I did four problems and got none of them right. Halfway into number five I got stuck again. I stared at the page. I asked God to send me the answer. He wouldn't. He was angry, I supposed, for my performance in Tanker's office. "I don't know," I said.

She pushed back from the table and crossed her legs. Sister Louise didn't have nun legs, which is what we called fat calves and ankles that shot straight into the shoes like the legs of a table. She had legs like a regular woman. She gave me half a stick of gum, and folded the other half into her mouth. Her lips were shiny and wet, as if she'd just put on lipstick.

I cupped my head in my hand and scribbled on my scratch paper. I looked out the window.

"You know," she said, "I was wondering how long it would take before you gave it to David Reilly. He's a little fresh mouth, that one." She gathered her books into a pile. "You've got to be more careful, though."

"I know. From now on I'll turn the other cheek."

"Turn the other cheek? Who fed you that line of garbage? Patrick, all I'm saying is, if you're going to beat him up, do it after school. And do it somewhere else. Take him down to the park, where nobody will see you."

She'd watched the fight, apparently, and she had pointers: always hit first, never look down or away, never cover up, never go beneath the other guy. "You did OK getting his shirt up and over," she said. "But you've got to hang onto it with one hand, and punch with the other."

She explained that she was a hockey fan. Her old boyfriend, she said, had been a hockey player, and he'd never lost a fight.

"You have a boyfriend?" I said.

"*Had*," she said. "I *had* a boyfriend."

"When?"

She looked out the window. "A long time ago," she said. "And look—here's your mother."

Sure enough, there was the station wagon, exhaust steaming from its tail pipe like dragon's breath. I would have to hear the rest of the story some other time.

I sat in the car while Sister Louise talked to my mother. At first I was disappointed in Sister Louise for telling on me; of course it was her duty, but somehow I'd hoped she was different. But then I realized that she might indeed be different— because outside the car they both began to laugh. I cracked open the window just in time to hear Sister Louise say, "You should have seen him."

We went to DiBurro's, a restaurant up on Route 125, near the river. My mother ordered a Manhattan and a Caesar salad; I ordered sautéed lobster and a Coke.

She hadn't said a word about the fight. Instead she asked me how the math was going.

"It isn't," I said.

"This new math." She shook her head. "I think I'd flunk it, too." She sipped her drink. "How's Dad?"

I said he was fine.

"Is he drinking?"

"No." I thought of his Friday night poker games at the Hibernians. "Well, I don't think so," I said.

She told me she was going to spend two weeks at Lake Winnipesaukee that summer. She said maybe I'd like to go with her. I picked at my lobster and tried to imagine me and Dr. Freedman out on a boat. I imagined killing him and tossing his body overboard.

"I'll think about it," I said.

Then I told her I didn't feel good, and we left without having dessert.

At home my father stood in the doorway looking out at my mother's car. She flicked her high beams on and off. He walked down off the porch as I was walking up.

I never asked how he felt about the situation, and I'm sure he would not have explained. My father built and repaired machinery, and although he would talk for hours about the ingenuity of tapered gears or the magic of arc welding, he would not say one word about his feelings for my mother. One afternoon when we were raking leaves for the landlord he told me that my mother and Dr. Freedman had gone to Bermuda for the weekend. How he'd learned this, I don't know. "Imagine that," he said. "Thursday night they talk about it, Friday afternoon off they go." Then he sat down on the back steps and began to cry.

I pulled back the shade and watched them talking in the car. They were nothing more than shadows. They were smoking, and the tips of their cigarettes glowed like fireflies. He was a fool, I thought. He had no pride, no shame.

When he came back in from talking to her I was at the

kitchen table, trying to find the least common denominator of fifty-seven and seventy-six. I tried three.

"Mom said you had a nice dinner," he said.

I tried four. No luck.

"Patrick?"

I tried five.

"Pat," he said. "Come on."

I tried six, thinking, *This could take forever.*

He put his hand on my shoulder. I wouldn't look up. I tried seven, then eight. They didn't work either. I looked at my paper, covered with worked-out multiplications, all mistakes. I put down my pencil. My hands shook. All these numbers, spinning in front of me. I was stupid—why was I stupid? I thought I might cry. Then I did cry. I was never going to figure this out.

A few days after our fight Reilly started up again—this time it was during gym—and afterward I trapped him in the lavatory and held his head in a toilet. A few minutes later, as Constance dragged me toward Tanker's office, I thought about public school: there were no uniforms, and they had real science labs with beakers and Bunsen burners and frogs to be dissected. I would have to make all new friends.

They kept me in Tanker's office all afternoon. Tanker wanted to get my mother to come to school so we could all talk together. But they couldn't find my mother. "Figures," Constance said, and stormed out. Tanker tried to reach my father, but there were only two places he'd be—the mill or the Hibernians—and I knew he wouldn't come to the phone at either one. When school ended the other kids marched out, and Sister Louise came in. Tanker said she had a meeting and she asked Louise to stay with me. On her way out the door Tanker said, "I'm disappointed in you, Patrick."

Sister Louise crouched down to take a book from the bottom

shelf of the bookcase; her skirt strained against her hips, and the front of her blouse buckled, allowing me a quick glance at the edge of her brassiere. She turned to me and I looked away, hoping she hadn't seen me looking. "OK," she said. "Get out your math book."

We tried dividing a fraction by a fraction, but it was hopeless. Finally I threw down my pencil and told her what I'd been wanting to say all along: "Sister," I said, "math is stupid."

She sighed and closed her book. "Patrick," she said, "math is pure. Everything else is wishy-washy. You take English, or history, or even religion, and people are always saying, 'Well, there's no right or wrong answer.' With math, there's always a right answer. If there's a problem, you can solve it. You're right or you're wrong. Life—well, life is messy. But math is pure."

"OK," I said. "But I still can't do it."

She said we should go to the convent to call my mother. Outside the air was cool, and there was a smell of leaves burning. She pulled her sweater across her chest.

When we got to the crosswalk at Andover Street I asked her if they were going to expel me.

"I hope not," she said. "I'd miss you."

"You would?"

She put her hand on my shoulder. "You remind me of someone," she said. "That hockey player in Nova Scotia."

"The one who got into fights, right?"

"That's right."

Over and over I'd imagined him: small, scrappy, maybe missing a tooth. But a good guy, a clean player. And I was like him, I thought. She took my hand to lead me across the street. I felt a flickering inside me.

We were moving down the narrow alley between the church and the rectory, so close our bodies bumped together, when she told me she had a little brother.

"He's just a little boy," she said. "He's with my parents. And I don't think you'd like him."

"I'd like him," I said.

"He has red hair. Like Virginia Brighton."

We were standing in the pool of light from the lamp above the convent door. "I can wait out here," I said.

She smiled. "Don't be silly," she said.

The convent was warm and the air was filled with the smell of steam and food cooking. We entered through a dark hallway lined with holy pictures. Inside to the right was the kitchen, where two nuns were working at the stove. To the left was a dining room with places set around a big wooden table, and down a narrow hallway toward the back was the den. As we approached the den I heard hoofbeats and gunshots and Michael Landon's voice calling for help, and when we got to the den my suspicion was confirmed: the Huns were watching "Bonanza."

They were crowded into the room. Not only were they watching television, but they had Cokes and potato chips on folding metal TV tables, and some were smoking. Constance was at the far end of the couch with her shoes off and her feet up on a hassock. Her feet were enormous.

Sister Louise had her arm around me, and with my shoulder I could feel the side of her body beneath her habit. The nuns smiled and said hello. They were happy old birds, I thought. But who wouldn't be, with nothing to do but watch television and drink Cokes and wait for your dinner to be ready? The Huns, I decided, had it made.

We went upstairs. Sister Louise opened the door to her room and told me to wait there while she called my mother.

I sat sideways on the edge of the chair at Sister Louise's desk. Her room was smaller than my room at home. There was one window, which looked out into the side yard. Against one wall was a bed with a wooden crucifix hanging above it. Beside the bed was a low table with a lamp. At the foot of the bed was a wooden dresser, with a guitar leaning against the side. The desk where I sat was small, like a little girl's desk, and the only things on it were a hairbrush, a box of baby powder, and a drinking glass. I imagined her coming back from a shower and putting baby powder on her arms. I imagined her waking up in the middle of the night and getting out of bed to get a drink of water.

The desk had a slim drawer across the top. I was not much of a sneak, and I certainly wouldn't steal anything, but I wondered, what does a nun keep in her desk? I pulled the drawer open slightly, just an inch or so, close enough that I could snap it shut if she came back.

There were some pens, an envelope, and some keys. There was also the corner of a photograph in a metal frame with a glass cover. I listened for a second. She was still talking. I opened the drawer and lifted the photograph out.

Tucked into the corner of the frame was a small black-and-white snapshot of a baby. He was sitting up, with his little fat legs sticking out of a pair of shorts. The framed photograph was a color picture of a family crowded around a picnic table. At the end of a bench was Sister Louise, wearing a pair of shorts and holding the red-headed baby. There was something wrong about the photograph, something wrong about Sister Louise. I looked again and realized what it was: her hair was red.

The door swung open. "Well, I left messages everywhere," she said.

I dropped the photograph into the drawer. She stood with a stunned look on her face, as if I'd just slapped her.

"You opened my drawer? You looked through my desk?"

"I didn't see anything."

She picked up the photograph. "You saw this, didn't you?"

"I'm sorry. I'm really sorry. I mean, I saw the picture, and I wanted to see if you were in it—you know, before you . . . before you came here."

I was shaking.

"OK," she said. "It's OK." She picked up the photograph. "It's all right."

She ran her fingers over the picture frame. She looked out the window, down into the yard.

I said, "That's you, right? The one on the end."

"Yes."

"That's what you look like?"

She turned to face me. "Here, you may as well see," she said, and before I knew what was happening she reached up and lifted off her veil. Her hair was bright red, and cut short, like a boy's.

"Well?" she said. "What do you think?"

I didn't know what to say. "I'm sorry," I blurted out. Then I said, "I mean, not for you. I just mean I'm sorry. I mean about this and Reilly and everything, and what I said about Virginia Brighton and—"

"Patrick, you have to stop being sorry all the time."

"Yes, Sister." I looked at the photograph. She was standing close to me. "You must hate me," I said.

"Of course I don't." She pinned her veil back onto her head, then looked into the mirror. "You made a mistake."

"I make a lot of mistakes."

"You do. But you don't hate people for their mistakes, Patrick. If you did you'd have to hate everyone, wouldn't you?"

"I guess so."

"Even yourself. You'd have to hate yourself—right?" She put the photograph back into the drawer, then leaned over, took my face in her hands, and drew me so close to her that I could feel her breath on my cheeks. Her hands were cool; her eyes were remarkably blue. She spoke in a near whisper. "Patrick," she said, "no matter what you did, I would still love you."

Her lips were no more than an inch from mine.

"Do you understand?" she said.

I was dizzy. I tried to say yes, I did understand. But all I could do was nod.

She let go of my face and stood up. "Well, come on, then. You're having dinner with us."

"Here?"

"Well, you've got to eat dinner."

Dinner with the Huns, I thought. Jesus. On the way down the stairs I stopped. "You know," I said, "I don't really think Virginia Brighton is gross. I really feel, well, the other way."

She smiled and said, "I know that, Patrick."

No joy can compare to the joy with which two dozen hungry nuns devour a huge, hot meal. They passed wine around the table, and big pitchers of ice water, and the platters of meat and vegetables came down the line in what seemed like a never-ending chain of food. As each platter came by Sister Louise would fill my plate until finally I had before me a small mountain of boiled potatoes and carrots, a wedge of cabbage, three slices of beautiful red corned beef and four gray-white spare ribs that extended off the end of my plate. Constance watched from across the table, and with each platter, as the mountain on my plate grew, the expression on her face became more horrified.

"Are you sure you've got enough?" Sister Louise said. She poured a trickle of vinegar onto my cabbage. "You let me know when you want seconds." She looked around the table. "Now where's the mustard? There. Sister Constance, would you pass the mustard?"

Constance scowled and passed the jar, and Sister Louise

spread a thick line of brown mustard on my corned beef. She watched my water glass as we ate, and each time it got half empty she filled it back up. One time, as she leaned over in front of me, I noticed a bit of red hair ducking out from the edge of her veil.

She had just loaded me up on seconds when the phone rang in the front room. A nun came in, looked at Sister Louise, and pointed to me. We went to the living room. The nun handed me the phone.

"I'm at a pay phone," my mother said. There were voices in the background.

"Where are you?"

"At DiBurro's. Are you OK?"

"I'm in a convent," I said.

"Have you had dinner?"

"We're having it right now."

"What are you having?" She had been drinking.

"Corned beef and cabbage."

She drew on a cigarette. "We'll be over to get you soon. Wait a minute. Here."

"Pat," my father said.

"Dad?"

"We've got some good news, Pat." He'd been drinking too. "Some real good news."

"Oh," I said. "OK."

I went back to the table, but I couldn't eat. I felt as if I'd been hit on the head with a baseball bat. The nuns brought out coffee and ice cream and blueberry pies. Sister Louise gave me a slice of pie with two scoops of ice cream on top.

"I can't," I said.

"Try," she said. "Just try some."

The nuns started going off to their rooms. One of them said

something about doing homework and I thought, maybe being a nun wouldn't be so great after all.

A few minutes later a car swung into the lot outside. Its headlights cast across the rectory and the church, then fixed on the convent. Sister Louise got my corduroy coat and my book bag.

I saw the silhouettes of my mother and father. I saw the glow of my mother's cigarette. She was sitting over close to my father. I admit I felt a melting in my heart, but I wondered how, after all this, could he sit there with her? How could he kiss her again, without thinking about Dr. Freedman? How, when someone hurts you, can you open your heart to them again? But there it was, my father's soul inviting meanness back in, like a church opening its doors to the devil. And here was Sister Louise, after all I'd done to her and to everyone else, stuffing me with ice cream and pie.

It seemed to me then that forgiveness was not an act of will, but rather something that couldn't be helped; that people had no choice but to forgive each other. This was not because they were good, but because they were bad; the soul was a place where meanness and evil were welcome guests. My father was getting what he deserved, and so was my mother.

"Have you got everything?" she said.

I nodded.

"Then go," she said. "Don't make them wait." I ran out across the headlights. My mother opened the front passenger door and in the sudden burst of light I saw their faces, smiling. I slid in on the front seat beside them.

Brothers

THE BOUNCER had broken Jimmy D'Amato's nose and left him face down in the parking lot. Maria got to him first, and her expression when she rolled him over made my heart sink: she was in ecstasy. Blood rose in her cheeks, her eyes seemed to glow; she held Jimmy in her arms as if he'd just been taken down off the cross, and I knew that whatever chances I might have had with her were gone.

Steve and I carried Jimmy to the car. On the way to the hospital Maria cradled his head in her lap and told him his nose didn't look so bad, although really the cartilage appeared ready to burst through the skin, the left nostril had disappeared, and the whole center of his face was turning marbly green-black and swelling like a balloon filling with water. The fight had not lasted long enough to be called a fight; it had been more like Jimmy throwing himself in front of a truck. The bouncer, Robert Fenton, stood a half foot taller than Jimmy and out-weighed him by a hundred pounds.

"I'm a kill'm," Jimmy said, his voice slurred and thick.

Steve rolled his eyes. Steve was my older brother, and for years he'd told me stories about Jimmy; now I was seeing for myself.

"I'm a kill'm," Jimmy said again.

"That's right, we'll get him," Maria said. "We'll get him back."

"We?" Steve said. "Who's *we?*"

She scowled. Her silk blouse was soaked with blood, and the fabric stuck to the curve of her breasts in a way that I found strangely erotic; I was seventeen years old and everything in those days seemed strangely erotic. There was blood on her hands and on her neck and a small smudge on the left side of her face. It was August, during a heat wave; she was sweating, and her sweat was mixing with the blood, and I found that erotic, too.

We waited three hours for the doctors to fix Jimmy's nose. Steve slept. Maria smoked. I watched her smoke and tried to think of things to say to her; but all my ideas were stupid, so finally I shut up and pretended to read an old edition of *Newsweek*. Near dawn Jimmy emerged with two black eyes and a strip of tape across the bridge of his nose. We drove downtown to Morin's Diner, where we ordered home fries and pancakes and coffee, and began to plan our revenge.

Maria Mendez was a Catholic boy's dream: good and bad, virgin and whore. On one hand, she went to St. Mary's and wore a white veil to Mass and kept a set of black rosary beads in her bedroom. On the other hand, she worked in a leather factory, wore red lipstick, and liked very much to show off her body when she danced.

She was a tease, and if she needed a ride home she would not think twice about pretending to like the boy with the car. She never said please or thank you, and she never gave more than a kiss goodnight. "You can do those things with other girls but not with me," she told Steve one night as she hopped out of his car, leaving behind a scent of flowery perfume which lingered on the seat for days.

She left Steve for Jimmy; but she would not sleep with Jimmy, either. What kept Jimmy going was that Maria always acted as if she were on the verge of changing her mind. Every time they went out, just as things got going she would find some ridiculous thing to get upset about—the way he combed his hair, the shirt he was wearing—and would refuse to go through with it. I wondered how long Jimmy would keep chasing her. Steve said Jimmy wouldn't ever give up. "Sooner or later he's going to get fed up," he said. "And when that day comes—" he smacked his hands together, "watch out."

Maria lived with her parents on Park Street, in the heart of the Puerto Rican ghetto, but she told me that she wouldn't be living there forever. She was saving money to go to community college; she was going to study business.

"What about you?" she asked me. "What are you going to study?"

"Classics," I said.

She looked at me.

"Latin," I explained. "Latin and Greek."

She made a face. "The hell you going to do with that?"

I said I didn't know.

Maria was my age—seventeen—but unlike the other girls I knew, who stumbled on their high heels, smeared their makeup, and acted as if they'd just discovered their breasts and hips and still didn't know what to make of them, at seventeen Maria had been in a woman's body long enough to know how to move in it. One day she asked me to take her to the driving range in Edmunds and show her how to hit a golf ball. She made me stand with my arms curled around under her breasts and my hips nestled up against her. Soon I felt myself reacting the way you might expect a boy to react, and I stepped away.

She looked over her shoulder and said, "What's the matter? You're not having fun?"

"No, I am," I said.

She smiled and said, "Yeah, maybe a little too much, right? Come on."

I hesitated.

"Come *on*," she said.

I got behind her again and this time she pressed herself against me and rolled her hips in a way that could only have been on purpose. I realized what she was doing.

"She's evil," Steve said later, when I told him.

"She's a tease, that's all," I said.

"No," he said. "She's evil."

Maybe he was right. Maria was, in fact, the reason that Jimmy got into the fight with the bouncer; she told Jimmy that the bouncer was calling her names and grabbing her. Steve said she wanted to see how far she could push Jimmy; she wanted to see someone fight over her. "You saw how she looked," he said. "She loved it. She's sick."

Jimmy was no better. He'd spent two years in the Marines and still wore his hair in a razor cut and said that the Corps, as he called it, was the best thing that ever happened to him. He was always telling me that I should enlist, and when I'd remind him that I was going to college he'd frown and say, "Well, Frank, suit yourself."

We worked at Pahigian's Garage on South Union Street, which for Steve and Jimmy was a real job but for me was a way to make spending money for what my father called "these days of wine and roses." The gas station was a small place near the Essex Street housing projects, with two gas islands and a pair of abandoned repair bays. The owner had given up on the place; he came by every evening to collect the cash drawer and receipts, but otherwise we were on our own.

And it was there, a week after the fight at the Admiral, that Jimmy told us that he and Maria had come up with a way to get Fenton back.

"We wait for him to come out of the bar," he said. "We follow him home, we grab him, we put him in the trunk of the car, and take him out to the woods someplace."

"And then what?" I said.

He looked at me. "What do you think?"

"I don't know."

He grinned at Steve and Maria, then looked back at me. "We all sit down and have a little talk," he said.

For days, then, the Fenton plan became our obsession. We spent hours going over details, looking for problems, things that could go wrong. To me this was no more serious than a math problem: *Given that X represents the task of hunting someone down and hurting him, and that A, B, and C are the obstacles, solve for X.*

There were two flaws, as I saw it. First was the initial encounter—getting him into the trunk—and second was being able to do everything without getting caught.

"Do we wear ski masks?" I said. "Pantyhose?"

"I vote for pantyhose," Steve said.

"You would," Jimmy said.

Jimmy said we wouldn't have to worry about being identified, since Fenton wouldn't remember anything when we were done. And as for getting Fenton into the car, he said, kicking a man in the groin, no matter how big he was, had a tendency to double him over. He demonstrated with a shot to the metal desk, which boomed and shuddered and made my skin go cold. Once, fooling around, Jimmy had cornered me out in the bays and started circling me like a boxer, flashing his fists at my arms and face. "I'm a Green Beret," he said, "and I'm going to kill you. We're alone in the woods. What do you do?" I covered my face; he punched my arms until they went numb. Steve stood at the edge of the bay, saying, "Come on, Jimmy, cut it out."

Sometimes to amuse himself Jimmy would slap Steve, and Steve would sit there, his hands at his side, afraid to hit back, saying, "Come on, Jimmy. Come on, Jimmy," and trying to laugh as his cheeks reddened from being hit. I did not like to watch this, but I knew Steve would feel even more embarrassed if I stepped in and tried to stop it.

I was disappointed to see Steve this way; but not surprised. There was a weakness about him, a missing piece, that had drawn him to Jimmy in the first place. What he wanted, secretly, was to *be* Jimmy.

Jimmy never flinched, never backed down, never didn't get what he wanted. Or so it seemed. He claimed he'd had thirty women, and this seemed possible: he had black hair and green eyes set deep in an angular, dangerous face. Still, it was hard to tell how much of Jimmy was talk and how much was real. He claimed, for example, that he'd killed a man in a bar fight in the Philippines and that the Marines had covered it up. Steve did not believe this, but I did, and the reason I did was that Jimmy claimed he had enjoyed it. If he'd said how awful it was I'd have known he was lying. But when he told that story, when he described the look on the Filipino's face, he smiled and his pupils grew so wide that the green irises almost vanished. "Frank, you feel it," he said. "You feel the life go out of him. It's amazing."

He was bad and crazy, and he seemed to know more about life than I ever would. I had never slept with a girl, had never been in a fight. I knew Latin and Greek, had read Virgil, Catullus, and Livy, and yet I envied people like Jimmy and Maria, who pumped gas and worked in leather factories.

My father was the son of a millwright, and he had worked summers in the Osgood Mill when he was younger, and he scoffed at the folk singers and poets who came to Lawton Falls for the Labor Day festival. The only people who thought that mill work was romantic, he said, were people who'd never done any. "You can't imagine," he said. "And thank God you can't. Go away. Forget this place."

Fenton came out of the Admiral at one thirty. He was alone. We followed him along the river road into the city, staying close behind him. Steve worried that we might lose him; Jimmy said not to worry, there was nobody else around. "Stay back a little bit," he said. He was smoking a cigarette, looking both ways at the cross streets and checking for police. Maria sat in back with me. She had not spoken much all night, and now that the plan had become real—now that we were actually "in pursuit," as Jimmy said—she seemed to have lost her nerve.

The streetlights downtown shone harsh and yellow, and in the glare the storefronts and brick office buildings stood out sharp against the shadows in the alleys. We followed Fenton down Essex Street and across the Broadway bridge into South Lawton, turned onto Amesbury Street, and then began to speed up, so that when Fenton turned into his driveway we pulled in right behind him.

Steve cut the headlights. He reached over the seat and took the Louisville Slugger that lay at my feet. Jimmy turned and looked over the seat at me and Maria and told us to be ready in case something went wrong. Then he reached under his seat and took out a revolver.

"Wait a minute," Steve said. "What the hell is this?"

But Jimmy had already opened his door.

"Jesus Christ," Maria said. "He's out of his mind."

From inside the car it was like watching a silent movie. Fenton smiled at first, and then he saw who it was and became angry. Then he saw the gun and his eyes went soft. They walked him around to the back of the car.

Maria and I sat tensed up in the back seat, waiting to hear the gun blast.

"Knock him out," Jimmy said.

Steve said something about the light in the trunk, and about the neighbors.

"Hit the goddamn guy," Jimmy said.

There was a crack, and then a thud. The car sagged on its springs as they placed Fenton into the trunk. Maria squeezed my arm and said, "Jesus, Jesus, Jesus," under her breath.

Steve and Jimmy got into the front seat. Steve started the engine, but didn't put the car in gear. We sat in the driveway.

"We can go now," Jimmy said.

Steve's face was red; he looked ready to cry. "What the hell is the gun?" he said. "What the hell is that? Have you got the goddamn thing loaded?"

Jimmy slid the gun under the seat and said, without looking at Steve, "I said we can go now."

We drove out Route 125 and headed north toward the missile base. Maria sat close to me, so close that I could smell her perfume, and when she shifted in the seat her bare thighs made a peeling sound against the car seat and I felt myself getting hard. She had shown up that afternoon wearing frayed denim shorts and a halter top that barely contained her. Now, in the moonlight, her dark skin seemed even darker, and her curly black hair shone, and her eyes were wide and dilated with excitement; they glistened like drops of motor oil. Soon the buildings grew farther apart, the woods became thicker, and as we moved beyond the limits of the city a salty taste began to thicken on my tongue. There was a thump from the trunk, and then another one.

I tapped Jimmy on the shoulder. "He's awake," I said.

He turned down the stereo. Fenton was pounding on the trunk lid.

Maria said, "Let's just drive him around for a while. You know, just scare him. We can leave him out at the quarry, like without his clothes or something."

Jimmy turned and stared at her. His face was black and swollen around his eyes, as if he were wearing a mask.

"You got us into this," he said.

Then he turned around and raised the volume on the stereo and looked straight ahead at the road.

The quarry was at the far southern edge of North Edmunds, past the subdivisions and the farms and the town forest. The site was a ten-acre dirt clearing with a hole in the middle which years before had filled with water. The water was deep and dark, and around it was a flat dirt clearing, as dry as the surface of some empty planet. Around the periphery were thick woods.

The main access road was blocked by a fence, but we left the paved road and took a rutted access road that led onto the quarry from the side; we drove out onto the clearing under a bright moon which lay a white stripe across the black water. Coming out of the woods it seemed as if we had crossed some threshold and had entered a new world where there was no one watching and where anything might happen. The tires of the car coughed up a cloud of dust that hung in the air behind us.

We stopped at the edge of the woods.

Jimmy reached under the seat and took out the revolver. The gun was real: a short blue-black barrell, brown wooden grips, fluted chambers, and a tiny sight, like half a penny, at the end of the barrel.

He started to open the door, but Maria reached over the seat and grabbed his neck and said, "Jimmy, come on. Put it away."

Jimmy freed himself and reached for his door, but she grabbed him again.

"Jimmy," she said. "We didn't come out here to kill anyone."

Jimmy looked out the side of his eyes at her hand on his neck.

"And what if it goes off or something?" she said. "You never know."

Jimmy smiled. "Yeah, you never know," he said. "OK." He leaned forward and put the gun back under the seat. Then he turned to me and said, "Give me the bat."

Jimmy stood beside the car, like a batter standing at the plate waiting for a pitch, while Steve put the key into the trunk lock and got ready to open the lid. Maria and I stood a few feet away. Fenton had been silent for a long time now and I had a feeling that he had suffocated. I imagined him curled up beside the spare tire, his face gone blue. But when the lid opened he sprang out of the trunk like a bull coming out of a rodeo stall.

Jimmy swung the bat into his stomach and doubled him over. He staggered, but then he grabbed Steve around the waist and drove him backward into the car. Steve hit the fender with a thud, and went limp. I grabbed Fenton's hair and got a couple of shots into his face—there was blood, my hand came back wet, and adrenaline rushed through me like a drug—but he drove his knee up into my stomach and I fell to my knees, feeling as if all the oxygen had been sucked from the air around me.

Then Jimmy cracked him across the back of the head and it was over. He fell like a bag of sand. "There," Jimmy said. "Good night."

I got back to my feet, feeling dizzy, wanting to retch. Fenton lay stretched out like a corpse. Even on his back he was huge. Jimmy reached under Fenton's shoulders and managed to lift him a few inches off the ground. Fenton's giant head lolled to the side.

"Let's go," Maria said.

"We're not done yet," Jimmy said.

"This is sick," she said. "I'm not watching this."

She got back into the car.

We dragged Fenton into the woods and took turns kicking

him. We started on his chest and back, then moved down to his legs. At first Fenton would groan each time we kicked him, and his little sounds, as awful as they were, made me angrier. But then he stopped making noise and I could not go on. I told them that my foot had begun to hurt.

"You shouldn't have worn sneakers," Jimmy said.

He and Steve wore steel-toed work boots. Steve kicked with the side of his foot, like a soccer player, but Jimmy used the toepiece. He kicked and cursed and jumped at Fenton like a man possessed. He'd gone over the edge, and the more he kicked the angrier he became. His eyes burned with a rage so fierce and so deep that it could not have been meant only for Fenton; no single person could merit so much hatred. He smelled of hatred. It was as if a well of madness and violence had been swelling in him all his life, and now at last it had been released.

Finally he stopped and stood there, his chest heaving, his face and neck coated with sweat. Steve stopped too.

Jimmy caught his breath and seemed to become calm. He spat on Fenton's face, and watched the spit trickle down across his cheek. So there, I thought. That's it.

But then Jimmy drove the toe of his boot into the spot where his spit had landed. There was a wet sound, like an egg cracking. I looked away, but too late: my stomach tightened, and I went into the woods and got sick.

When I came out they were gone. Fenton was alone. His hair and shirt were thick with blood. They had gone after his face, and now he didn't seem to have a face anymore. He looked dead; but I could hear his breath rising in shallow spurts.

From the clearing I heard Maria shriek. Then I heard Jimmy shout, "Give me back the gun."

When I stepped out of the woods Jimmy was standing by the pond, facing Maria. Steve stood behind Jimmy. Both of them were soaked to the knees in blood: their shoes, their jeans. Maria stood facing them, a few feet away. She was holding the gun in her right hand. She held it away from her body, as if she were afraid to let it touch her.

"We're not killing anybody," she said. She began to back away from them.

But in fact we *were* going to kill Fenton; at least if Jimmy had his way. I remembered his story about the Filipino, and then I understood the truth of what he'd brought us here to do.

"Look—" I said.

Jimmy turned toward me and in that instant Maria cocked her arm and threw the pistol out over the water. Jimmy sprang at her and knocked her over; she fell to the ground with him on top of her.

The gun flew clumsily, tumbling sideways, and plopped into the pond and disappeared. That sound, that plop, rang across the clearing and seemed to hang in the air, and when Maria replays this night in her memory I am sure that she hears that sound and remembers it as the sound of her luck turning bad; she must go over and over that decision and know that she could have saved herself by simply handing over the gun and letting Fenton die. Because that was the moment when things changed in a way that none of us could have expected.

Jimmy picked her up and dragged her back to the car, where Steve and I were standing. She pulled herself free and said to Jimmy, "I just kept you from spending your life in jail. You should thank me."

He looked at her; the corners of his mouth began to curl up into a smile.

"You know," he said, "you're right."

He struck her in the face so hard that she fell to the ground. When she stood up a stream of blood ran from the corner of her mouth. She looked down at her feet.

"You take me home now," she said, in a quiet voice. "And then I don't ever want to see you again."

She walked to the car and got into the back seat. There was a long moment when none of us spoke, and everything became still, and I felt a terrible energy gathering in the air around us.

"Let's get out of here," I said.

They stared at the car, as if they hadn't heard me, as if I didn't exist. Then they walked to the car. Jimmy got in back with Maria. Steve and I got in front. Maria sat with her legs pressed together, biting her lip, staring down at the floor; Jimmy sat beside her, seething. Steve put the keys into the ignition, then leaned over the wheel.

"Steve," I said, "start the car."

But again it was as if I weren't there. We sat for a long time, in silence. Steve smoked a cigarette. When he was done he snapped the butt out his window and looked into the rearview mirror at Jimmy. As if on cue, Jimmy grabbed Maria's hair and snapped her head against the seat and said, "You know, I've had it with you."

She said, "It's over, Jimmy. Forget it."

"No," he said. "It's not over."

Steve climbed into the back and the two of them began to take off her clothes. She did not struggle; she seemed to know there was no use. She was not wearing much clothing, and in a few seconds she was naked, her face blank and tilted up, her eyes fixed on the roof of the car; she looked as if she were praying. Jimmy knelt behind her and held her arms. Steve knelt between her legs and as he began to open his pants he turned and looked at me. His eyes were heavy-lidded and serious, as if he were about to do some boring piece of work. He seemed to be about to say something, but he didn't.

Maria followed his gaze and turned her head to face me. In a voice that was nearly a whisper, she said, "So what about you?"

I knew what I should do. I knew that what was happening was wrong. And the only reason I can give for my failure is this: in some part of myself—at some low, deep level that I had not known existed—I knew why they were doing this to Maria, because I wanted to do it, too.

I did not hate her. I was not angry at her for being a tease. But I wanted to get into the back seat; I wanted to touch her. I feared her, and perhaps I loved her—maybe those two are not so different—and the sight of her scared and naked, the muscles in her neck tensing, her face tight, her arms and legs coiled and beginning to struggle: these things excited me.

I said, "I'm getting out of the car."

Jimmy said something about me being a virgin for the rest of my life, and Steve laughed. Maria's face began to shake so badly that I couldn't look at her anymore.

I got out and walked into the woods and stood in the dark among the trees. The moon was behind the clouds and the car was a dark shape, heaving on its springs. The springs made a rusty, creaking sound. I could not see Steve and Jimmy; only their shadows. Twice Maria cried out.

When it was over Steve and Jimmy stepped out of the car and there was a thin line of blood on the side of Steve's neck. The air smelled sweet. I felt sick again. The sky was thick and heavy with stars which appeared to be right on top of us. The trees seemed to tilt and huddle.

On the way home I sat in the back with Maria. She sat silent, looking straight ahead. She acted as if nothing had happened—as if we'd all been to the beach and had had too much to drink, as if the pink bruise on her cheek had come from bumping her head on the pier beneath the arcades. They had torn her shirt and now she held the pieces over her breasts and smoked one of Jimmy's cigarettes.

Steve and Jimmy talked about the Red Sox. Jimmy said, "You watch the Red Sox, Maria?"

She shook her head.

Fenton was back at the missile base. I wondered what would happen to him; I thought that maybe I should call the police. But these ideas rushed away as quickly as they came, and what I fixed on finally—what I held onto—was that in two weeks I would leave for college and never return; and in a few hours I would be at Mass and I could go to confession and have this wiped away.

But as we drove back into the empty city, where the streetlights were blinking yellow and the stores stood dark behind their metal grids, I knew that although we had come back across the threshold, we had not returned to a world of order, but instead had brought the emptiness of that other world back with us. I had a sense that even if I were to pray, my prayers would not be heard. And then a worse and further knowledge came to me: that my prayers had never been heard. My sins were my sins—mine. I closed my eyes and listened to the hum of the tires as we passed over the Canal Street bridge.

I knew even then that leaving this city and never coming back would not make a difference; that our failures remain with us, and define us, forever. What I could not know then, however, was the entirety of my failure. I'd failed Maria and failed myself; but I'd also failed Steve. Only years later, as I watched him buried without eulogy on a hill overlooking the river, would I remember his eyes in the car that night, as he knelt before Jimmy and Maria, and realize that I could have saved him.

I looked at Steve in the mirror. He wouldn't look back. The blood on his neck had dried into a thin red-brown line. His face had changed; his life had swung down, and maybe for good, like the arc of a thrown ball when it stops climbing and begins its descent.

Maria did not seem to care at all. I took her hand, but she slid it away and crossed her arms and sat there, looking out the window. When we stopped outside her house it was almost dawn. Music from a radio drifted out a window into the street: trumpets, guitars, a man's voice singing in Spanish.

I wished she would cry, or yell, or try to hit us. But she just got out of the car and closed the door. Jimmy said, "Good night, Maria," and she turned on the sidewalk and said, "Good night."

We watched her go up the inside stairs. I imagined her inside, naked, holding a cloth to her swollen face, taking a bath to wash us from her body, hoping that as long as she didn't get upset she might be able to believe that the whole thing had never happened.

Jimmy said we should drive to the beach to see the sunrise. Steve drove fast on the curves of the river road, and outside, on the river, mist steamed up and hovered in wisps over the water. The dark cottages, with their sad, small lives now sleeping, gained form in the gray light. In one house the lights were on and a man sat at a table; I imagined him woken by some bad news, then making coffee and sitting in the bare light, not wanting to take the news alone but knowing he would have to. Behind the cottages the river scraped at its banks, dislodging bottles and bags of trash which by that afternoon would snag in the canals and dams of the city.

"Steve," I said. "Stop the car."

He pulled over. We got out and walked to the back of the car.

"I'm going home," I said.

He glanced into the car at Jimmy, as if he were afraid of what Jimmy might hear. But Jimmy sat in the front seat, smoking, looking out at the river.

I said what I believed: that he had not wanted to do what he had done; that he had just been too afraid of Jimmy. Any reasonable person would understand that, I said. "They'll believe us," I said. "We can go together."

He looked in at Jimmy again. Then he looked at me and

shook his head. He seemed small and frightened, like a little boy lost in the rain.

"I can't," he said.

He shuffled his boot in the dirt, his bottom lip curled and trembled: he looked doomed.

I said, "I'm your brother."

"No," he said. "Not anymore."

He was right. We were headed in different directions; we had been all along.

He got back into his car and drove away. And then there was nothing—only the hot, sweet, empty air, the shivering trees, and the long low rush of the river. I turned and walked back toward the city, wondering what I would say.

The Last
Good Man

DAVIO GIACCALONE's eyes grew red and welled with tears as he told me the story. "Jerry," he said, "we're talking Hiroshima here."

There is nothing like watching a crook find religion. His nose twitched, his eyes blinked: he looked hurt and innocent and naive, pained by the horrible thing he was about to tell me.

"There was a bribe," he said. "I can prove it."

We were in the Krakow Lounge, a blue-collar bar on the north side of the city. It was October, late in the afternoon. The room was full of ham-faced Polack millwrights, drinking beer and playing Forty-fives with decks of greasy cards. Sawdust on the floor, a game show on TV, the uriney odor of textile dye and sweat: I gathered in all these things, rolled the ice in my glass of Jameson's, and considered again the sour taste of my professional decline.

"Davio," I said, "just say what you have to say."

"One word." He smiled. "Tsunami."

"That's a pretty short story." I stood up and started for the door.

"Mr. Gallagher." He grabbed my arm. "Please. There's more."

Tsunami, he said, was Tsunami Industrial Company, Inc., a

Japanese computer company that was going to buy the Osgood Mill, lay off the mill workers, and use the building to set up a robotic assembly plant. "They're not really robots," he said. "They're just these arms and stuff." He waved toward the tables of millwrights. "But the point is, Jerry, that every one of these guys gets a pink slip. The city's dead."

Two thousand people worked at the Osgood. It was the last working mill in the city. Even I could see how its demise could be turned into poetry: the end of the Industrial Revolution, the silenced mills stretched out like corpses on the banks of the filthy river, the sons of sons of sons of millwrights turned out into the crumbling streets.

"That's some story," I said.

"Wait," he said. "It gets better."

He produced a photocopy of Tommy Lynch's bank statement and a photocopy of a canceled Tsunami check for $50,000. The Japanese, he said, had paid Lynch, the mayor, to keep him from opposing the sale. "So the city goes to hell, and Tommy retires in Florida and washes his hands of the whole thing," he said.

The papers seemed authentic. "How'd you get these?" I said.

"Don't ask," he said, and took them back. "You'll have to trust me."

The thing is this: my job requires me to put faith in crooks. And strange as this seems, crooks are usually trustworthy. Some of the best stories I ever heard, in fact, came from people I wouldn't trust to park my car.

The best are crooks who want revenge. That's what Giaccalone was after, despite his concerned-citizen act. He'd been caught skimming from the pension fund of the Ladies Garment Workers Union (he was local president) and Lynch had leaned hard on the district attorney to prosecute. Giaccalone lost his job, his house, and his car; he'd served six months of a two-year sentence, and while he was away his wife had left him. He blamed it all on Lynch. And now he was getting even. He'd waited a long time for this moment.

I drove Giaccalone to the Sons of Italy Hall on Newbury Street. On the way he mentioned that Lynch and his aldermen were buying Osgood stock. Shares were trading at two dollars, but Tsunami was going to pay six a share, in a stock swap.

"They're bandits," he said.

I didn't say anything. We were parked in front of the Napoli bakery. It was late, and the light was going thin in the sky above the row houses. He started to open his door, then stopped.

"I only told you because I know you're clean," he said.

"Like the driven snow," I said.

He shrugged his jacket around his shoulders. "Jerry, you know, you wouldn't. . . ." He looked down at his hands. "What I mean is . . . well, with the stock. You know what I mean."

"Get out of the car," I said.

When I was seventeen years old I fell in love with a girl named Kathleen Dwyer. We planned to be married when I returned from the war. But while I was in the Pacific building a runway on the island of Tinian, Kathleen got involved with a football captain whose heart murmur had kept him out of the war. By the time the Enola Gay had flown off my runway and carved two giant ashtrays out of the Japanese landscape and made it possible for me to come home, my Kathleen was married and nursing a baby. Her husband's name was Tommy Lynch.

I tracked him down at the Hibernians one rainy night and dragged him out into the street. He was drunk, and he kept slipping on the wet cobblestones, but still he managed to thrash me. My friends had to carry me home.

I tried to put this behind me. I married Mary Levis, a plain girl who loved me more than I loved her. I went to work at the *Lawton Falls Gazette*. Tommy Lynch went into politics. Our careers rose in parallel. I became city hall reporter, he became an alderman. I became city editor, he became mayor.

We lived on Tower Hill, only a few blocks away from each other, and although our salaries were roughly the same, our life-styles were not. Mary and I lived modestly and put a little bit away each month, while the Lynch family—Tommy, Kathleen, and the seven children they eventually produced—owned two cars and a summer house at Salisbury Beach. One year, as if by magic, a swimming pool appeared in their backyard. There was talk of corruption. For years I tried, quietly, to undo him. I'm sure he knew this. Still, Mary and I were never excluded from the round of summer cookouts at the Lynch beach house. When we exposed a crooked judge or revealed that an alderman had padded the bills for winter salt and sand, Tommy mixed my drinks and didn't mention the stories. I smiled, drank his Scotch, and lay in wait for him.

Before I could give him the sword, however, I got it myself. I'd just been promoted to managing editor when the *Gazette* was sold to a Wisconsin newspaper chain which sent a new editor, a little whelp named Barry Minkow, who gave me a choice: take a job as a "public affairs editor," or take a gold watch. I could not afford to retire; I took the job.

I'd been a crusader—had ruined more than a few careers—and so plenty of people were glad to see me gone. The idea of a powerful man reduced to writing reminiscence columns, cover-ing elementary school Christmas pageants and country club dinners, snapping photographs of men who once feared him, asking their wives *And how much has the Andona Society raised this year?*—I assume that the humiliation of this does not need to be explained. I was moved out of the newsroom, to an "office" beside the photo lab: a little cement cave that once had been a darkroom and that still smelled faintly of developing solution. At parties Tommy Lynch would put his hand on my shoulder and tell everyone how he'd stolen Kathleen away from me, and I'd fake a smile, avoid looking at Kathleen, and hold up my glass for a refill.

Mary met me at the door when I returned home from my drink with Giaccalone. "Kathleen called," she said. "You'll never guess. She and Tommy are going on a cruise—to Tahiti. Tahiti!"

"Maybe there'll be a hurricane," I said, and hung up my coat on the rack in the front hall.

"Oh, Grumpy," she said. "Lighten up."

She laughed and kissed me and hurried back to the kitchen. She is a retired schoolteacher, and like many people whose lives have been difficult, she is blessed with the ability not to take life too seriously. Her eyes are green and clear, and she jokes a great deal, and when she laughs the patches of wrinkles at her temples expand and contract like the folds of an accordion. She chose to be a teacher because she loved children. The irony was that she could not have her own. When we learned this I hid my disappointment and told her that it made no difference; but each year, when another fat little Lynch baby sprang out of Kathleen's fertile womb, I felt anger and bitterness wind themselves tighter around my heart, like the strands of some wicked creeping plant.

During dinner Mary brought up the Lynches and their cruise again. "Ta-hi-ti," she said, drawing out the vowels as if she were saying a prayer. "Can you imagine?"

I could. For the rest of that evening, in fact, I sat alone in my study, haunted by the image of Tommy Lynch out on the deck of a cruise ship, wearing a Hawaiian shirt and doing the hula. Mary and I had savings and equity in the house, and I'd be getting a pension—but still retirement loomed over us like a cloud over a picnic. We weren't going to be taking any cruises.

We had $86,625 in the bank, most of it from passbook interest on her share in her parents' house, sold when they died twenty years ago. For the hell of it, I got out a calculator and worked out how many shares of Osgood stock I could buy with that money, considering fees and commissions: about forty thousand. Then I figured how much those shares would be worth after they'd been converted into Tsunami shares in the stock swap. The sum was astonishing. For a moment I just sat there, looking at the numbers.

I asked myself this question: At the end of an indistinguished career you are given the chance either to redeem yourself or to make a great deal of money in an illicit fashion. What do you do?

I have a Catholic education, and I consider myself a man of honor. But that night, alone in my study, I heard that money whispering to me.

Tommy Lynch had his feet up on his desk. All my life, whenever I saw him, my first instinct was to slap him. I'd never got rid of the picture of him and Kathleen lying together. But I checked my anger and sat down. I took out my notebook and a pen.

"So what can I do you for," he said.

I had planned to toy with him for a while; but when I began to speak my excitement overcame me and I rushed ahead and told him what I knew. My knees jerked. I held my notebook on my lap and my pen in my hand, but I trembled so much that I could not write.

This was the Grail, the Ark of the Covenant: a six-term mayor and I was about to crush him beneath my heel. Over breakfast that morning I'd imagined the next month or two: a series of articles on Lynch, with sidebars on aldermen who'd made deals with Tsunami; editorials calling for Lynch to step down; a recall drive, a special election, the city saved from the Mongol horde, throngs of millworkers storming city hall, carrying me on their shoulders. . . .

Lynch took his feet down from his desk. A line of sweat began to set up above his collar. The patches of veins bloomed in his cheeks. When he spoke his voice was soft, almost a whisper. "Jerry," he said, "I'm an old man, for Christ's sake."

I had expected a denial, an outburst, a flaring of lips and a gnashing of teeth, a fist in my face. But this? Rolling over and playing dead?

"Let's have a drink," he said.

He poured me a glass. I looked out the window. This was all wrong. The leaves on the common had turned; they lay on the ground like a quilt.

He came around his desk and put his hand on my shoulder. "Jerry," he said, "look—you want in on this?"

"Don't insult me," I said.

My words fell out with a thud. I felt as if my heart had been removed. I could not make myself angry.

I drained my glass and set it on his desk. He drained his, too.

"Anyway," he said, "the deal's done. Papers are signed. You're pissing into the wind. There's a press conference Friday at the Heritage Park."

I left without saying good-bye. I drove over the falls bridge and into South Lawton, the old Irish ghetto in whose streets I had played as a boy. O'Neil's Bar was now La Bahia, the St. Patrick Church was La Familia Sagrada, and the only trace of green was in the window of a shop called The Olde Sod Imports, a little place that sold Clancy Brothers records and miniature Blarney Castles.

Before I could get across the newsroom to my cave, Minkow had me cornered by the wire machine. "Jerry, for Christ's sake, it's ten o'clock," he said. "We're holding the afternoon opener for your piece on the Andona Club lunch. Did you remember to go?"

"Yes," I said.

In fact I had arrived early. The woman in charge had mistaken me for the caterer.

Minkow leaned toward me and wrinkled his nose. "Christ, Jerry," he said, "have you been drinking?"

"Go away," I said.

Minkow had turned the *Gazette* into some sort of Star Trek slave ship: molded plastic computer terminals, as smooth as coffin lids; no drinking, no smoking, no swearing. These weren't newspaper reporters—these were *journalists*. They fretted, fingered their thesauruses, and came up with words like "ameliorate." Or "assuage." And when the copy went to the desk and the grunts changed it back into English, the little piss-ants threw fits.

I finished the Andona story, then went back to the newsroom and watched Minkow working with one of his choirboy protégés, the two of them curled over a computer screen and sharing a bag of M&Ms. I imagined going to him with my Tsunami story. I imagined him listening, nodding his head, then calling in one of his little pals to poach my piece. Or maybe he'd nod his head and tell me I was crazy, and send me back to my cave.

All morning I'd been haunted by the memory of my father, who lived out the end of his life on an Osgood Mill pension. It had seemed impossible for him to grow old. But all of a sudden he had. And now, a moment later (or so it seemed) here was I, standing at the same station. I imagined myself like my father: wearing my one ragged sweater, smoking a cheaper brand of cigars.

And in the back of my mind that money was still whispering to me, drawing me forward like a hypnotist.

I went back to my office, locked the door, and called a man I know, a stockbroker named George Tine, and asked how I might go about buying shares in the Osgood. It occurred to me that placing a stock order was the kind of thing that any grown man who'd made a decent living would know how to do. *You see how you've shortchanged yourself,* the money whispered.

"Got some dope on the mill?" Tine said. "That it?"

"No," I said. "No dope."

"You just want to buy some stock in a run-down textile mill. Sentimental reasons, maybe."

"That's right."

He explained how I would open an account. There were some issues about taking the money from the IRA account, and some tax issues, but he could handle them. I could sign Mary's name for her. It could all be done in minutes.

"I suppose you've considered the risks," he said.

I told him I had. But now an image came to me: the deal gone sour, our money gone, the house sold, the two of us living in a condominium out beside Route 93. And then a further risk revealed itself—if caught, I would spend my golden years in a jail cell. My insides began to twitch and go cold. "George," I said, "I'll have to call you back."

At lunch I went to the Hibernians and drank a pint of black and two shots of Jameson's. I can be a devious man. I've made a living out of tricking people into saying things they shouldn't. But I am also a Catholic, and when I sin it is with knowledge of my sinfulness, and it isn't easy. Which is to say that even with a stomach full of Irish I found myself stammering when Tine picked up his phone.

"George," I said, "about that thing we talked about . . . the order I mean. . . ."

"You want to go with the Osgood."

"That's it."

I visited the bank, and then crossed the street to George Tine's office. An hour later I left with a receipt for forty thousand Osgood shares.

I spent the afternoon at the Hibernians, sipping just often enough to buoy the fine, sweet dullness. When I stepped outside night was falling and hundreds of workers flooded past me on the sidewalk, headed home. I tried to imagine the city in six months, or a year—the empty sidewalks, the clock gone dead over the First Essex Bank, plywood in the window of Kaplan's Clothing For Men.

The gas lamps on Canal Street glowed dimly against the dusking sky. Puddles of water shimmered in the old horse-and-carriage grooves in the cobblestones. I stopped at the railing and stood alone by the north canal, rubbing the thin elbows of my jacket. The gray water seemed not to flow at all. On all sides the mills loomed over me—brick walls, brick smokestacks, brick bell towers—a big brick fortress crumbling at the corners like a Roman ruin. The whole city seemed dreary and leftover and out of date; and I seemed small and cheap.

Back at the *Gazette* I played a few hands of Forty-fives with Max and the boys on the sports desk. When the last of them had gone home, I typed a resignation letter and slipped it under Minkow's door.

That night, Mary and I celebrated in a little French restaurant. There among the potted plants and classical music I was nervous and ashamed. I could not eat. Even after I'd got home to bed with the lights off and Mary in my arms I could not feel at ease. Outside I swear there were crickets chirping, and already my damnation had begun, for what I heard them singing was *thief, thief, thief. . . .*

A week later the blue-suited Japanese marched triumphant into Lawton Falls, and hung a Tsunami logo on the east wall of the Osgood. All but two hundred workers were laid off. We had a difficult winter, the worst since the Depression. The unemployment office opened an extra branch in the Heritage Museum to handle the flood of new cases. The Christmas season was marked by a rash of housebreaks and liquor store robberies. In February a wool sorter who'd lost his job killed his wife and daughter and then threw himself off the falls bridge.

I spent my days dawdling around the house, startled occasionally by the sound of a car outside. I'd rush to the window, certain that the police had come for me, and discover that it was just Mrs. Lannon from across the street, pulling into her driveway. Soon I stopped worrying about the police, but I could not put my swindle behind me. As if to taunt me, the Tsunami shares I'd got in the stock swap soared in value. At night, as I lay in bed, the events of my life paid out in my mind like line from a reel. Often I was unable to sleep.

One Sunday morning in March I read in the *Gazette* that Tsunami was going to enter the largest float in the St. Patrick's Day parade. The idea made me shudder. I flipped to the back pages, scanned through the little six-point numbers, and found that my Tsunami shares had gone up again: the little yellow bastards were doing a blazing business with their robots.

We went to the late Mass at St. Michael's. A young priest was hearing confessions. I got in line with three little Italian widows dressed in black shawls (what could their sins be?) and stared at a stained glass window that depicted Christ in the garden at Gethsemane.

When my turn came I discovered that this was to be an open confession—no screen, that is. But still I plunged ahead: "I have stolen," I said.

I bowed my head and closed my eyes and prepared to empty my soul. But the young curate was unfazed. "Three Hail Marys, three Our Fathers and an Act of Contrition," he said, and before I could interrupt he'd begun his blessing.

A few days later, when Mary was out running errands, I finally washed my hands of the deal: I called George Tine and had him sell my shares.

"Did pretty well on these, Jerry," he said. "Not bad for a first-timer."

"Beginner's luck," I said.

He told me that he'd followed my lead on the Osgood, and had bought a few shares himself. "Had a hunch about your hunch," he said. Then he laughed and said some things about nest eggs and paper trails and told me not to worry. "Jerry," he said, "this is between you and me and the lamp post, OK?"

The next day I restored the $86,625 to our account at the First Essex, then walked down the street to the Lawton Falls Savings Bank and put my profit—$193,500—into two new accounts.

I was in a booth at Morin's diner, reading the *Gazette* and picking at a plate of fish and chips, when Davio Giaccalone sat down across from me. I hadn't seen him since that night in October.

"So," he said. He took a french fry from my plate.

"So," I said.

His face seemed thinner than when I'd seen him last. Somewhere out back a phone was ringing.

"My brother lost his job at the Osgood," he said. "His kid dropped out of high school. He's using dope."

He took another french fry from my plate.

"I'm sorry," I said.

"Sure you are." He stood up and left.

Saturday night it was raining and cold, and I would have been happy to stay on the couch with a glass of Jameson's and the TV turned to college basketball, but Mary insisted that we go to the St. Patrick's Day dinner at the Hibernians. "It'll cheer you up," she said.

"The same old fools and the same old jokes," I said. "Lynch will do the one about the tinker on the motorcycle—"

"Enough already," she said. "Now get the umbrella and let's go."

A band was playing "The Bold Fenian Men," and the hall was decorated with green balloons and streamers. On the walls were photographs of Lawton Falls' Irish heroes—Digger Clancy, Johnny Minihan, Pat O'Neill—whose fine, clear eyes belied their true nature: Clancy had embezzled city money; Minihan had been a bootlegger; O'Neill had sold jobs in public works for a thousand dollars. No wonder I was a crook. I was descended from a long line of under-the-table operators. The latest was Tommy Lynch, who at that moment was standing at the dais with an "*Erin Go Bragh*" banner strung on the wall behind him.

"It's so good to see so many old friends here," he said. "I'm reminded of the tinker who was walking along the path and came upon a motorcycle. . . ."

I stood up to go to the men's room, but Mary took my arm. "Jerry, wait," she said. "One minute. Here, sit back down."

At the back of the room a dozen Japanese were sitting around a table, wearing green blazers. Lynch introduced them and said what great things they were doing for the city. People began to hiss. That afternoon the Tsunami float had been pelted with tomatoes.

"Now I know that this is St. Patrick's Day," Lynch said, "but, well, tonight's a little different." He looked at Mary. "What do you think—should we tell him?"

She nodded. I looked at her, and then at Lynch. All at once I realized what was happening.

"Jerry," he said, "this is a party for you."

I sat there, my head spinning, my face growing hot, while the room broke into applause and laughter. The girls from St. Michael's carried out corned beef and cabbage, and then served coffee and set a cake on a table at the front of the room. Minkow gave a curt speech, the state reps took turns roasting me, and then Lynch returned to the dais.

"The thing about Jerry," he said, "was that he never stopped caring about this city. . . ."

In the back Giaccalone stood by an open window, smoking a cigar. George Tine was sitting with his wife. Two tables over was the priest to whom I'd confessed. At last Lynch finished, and as the room burst into hollers and shouts I thought, fine, we'll let the applause drain off and I'll cut the cake and go home.

But then Mary got up and went to the stage. She adjusted the microphone. She took a speech from her pocket and put on her reading glasses. "I want to tell you about my husband," she began, her voice trembling. "I want you to know why, after forty-six years, I still love him as much as I did the day we were married."

My stomach flipped and rolled; I could not swallow. Max slid me a glass of whiskey, but I didn't dare drink it.

"It's not because he's a snappy dresser," she said. "He'd wear the same clothes every day, if it were up to him. His shoes are falling off his feet before he'll replace them. He cuts his own hair. God knows he's not the sunniest personality on the planet. And God knows he's made plenty of enemies over the years. But no matter what you say about Jerry, you have to say that he cared. His work meant everything to him. And seeing you all here tonight I know you're as proud to have known him as I am." She took off her glasses, looked at me for a moment, and said, "We love you, Jerry."

In small groups they rose. Kathleen Lynch was crying. Even Max Higgins seemed choked up. I tossed the Jameson's down my throat, feeling first the urge to gag and then the warmth in my stomach. Mary came down and hugged me. Her face was covered with tears. Lynch stood up at the microphone and I feared he was going to sing, as he sometimes did, and I just prayed that he wouldn't sing "Danny Boy," because that song, at that moment, would have destroyed me.

But instead he said, "Jerry, get up here and say a few words."

They cheered, but when I just stood there they began to grow uneasy, and finally an awkward silence fell over the room. The door to the kitchen swung open, then shut with a thump.

"I don't know what to say," I said. I tried to think of a joke. But none would come. Part of me wanted to tell them what I'd done. Imagine the reaction to that. What I said at last was, "You shouldn't have done this," and then I dashed for the back door.

"Jerry, for Christ's sake," Max said.

"It's all right," Lynch said over the loudspeakers. "Let's just let him catch his breath a little. I'm sure it's a little overwhelming. . . ."

I ran down the back stairs and out into the alley behind the building. Inside, Max was at the microphone, leading the room through the chorus of "My Wild Irish Rose." The voices echoed in the alley.

The rain had lightened to a drizzle. Still, I was getting wet through my jacket. I considered running out to Essex Street and hailing a cab for home. But then the door opened and out stepped Tommy Lynch, pulling on his raincoat.

"Christ, Jerry," he said. "It's raining out here." He looked at me and smiled in a shy way, as if he was embarrassed. We had not spoken to each other since that day in his office. How unlike ourselves we had become, I thought. How small and stooped and gray; how old. Only a moment ago, it seemed, we were twenty years old, standing outside this barroom in the rain, squared off.

We stood looking at each other for a moment.

"I suppose you know what I did," I said.

"Yes," he said. His voice was quiet; he sounded the way he had the last time I'd seen him. "It must have killed you, passing up a chance to crucify me."

"I suppose so," I said. I looked past him, down the alley, to where water poured from a spout into the gutter. I could not look at him.

"All these years," he said, "you've been trying to catch me at something. What's it been? Forty years?"

"Forty-four," I said.

"And all over Kathleen. You never figured it out," he said.

I told him that I figured plenty.

"No," he said. "You didn't." His voice rose. "You were too busy being bitter about what a goddamn tragedy your life was. The whole world was out to get you, right? And you took it out on all of us."

I was ready to take a swing at him. I didn't have to listen to this. "You can go on all night with your politician gab," I said, "but the truth is the truth. You stole my girl."

"Jerry," he said, "wake up. We *had* to get married, OK? Didn't you ever figure that out? We didn't want to get married—neither of us. Especially not her. We *had* to get married. We had no choice."

He turned to face me. His hair was drenched and stuck to his head. His face had become angry.

"She didn't love me," he said. "Not then, not ever. She loved you." He stepped toward me and I remembered that night when his big fist had flashed up at me. He grasped the sleeve of my jacket and said, "Do you understand now? Do you understand? Can you finally get it through your skull?"

My voice would not work. So instead I nodded and tried to catch my breath. We'd all lived the wrong lives, it seemed. And now, at the end, all the logic had been turned inside out, like an old jacket.

Tommy still held my arm. He stood so close to me that I could smell his breath. I was not ready to stop hating him.

"You're still a crook," I said. "You're a crook, and so am I. There's no getting around that."

He was breathing hard. His chest rose beneath his raincoat as if he'd just run a mile. I thought about that bad heart of his, and imagined him keeling over out here in the rain. He took my hand.

"Jerry," he said, "come here."

He led me out of the alley. We stood under the awning in front of the army-navy surplus store. Essex Street was covered with litter from the parade. The rain made a pattering sound on the street.

He pressed his palm against the display window of the army-navy store. When he stepped away his handprint steamed, then faded and was gone. "You see?" he said.

"No," I said.

He took my hand and pressed the palm against the glass. He pulled my hand away, but kept hold of my wrist. I wondered what someone might think, seeing two old men holding hands on Essex Street. I didn't let go, though.

"You see?" he said.

I watched my palm print evaporate and vanish from the glass. "Yes," I said. "Yes I do."

I looked down Essex Street, past the stores and bars and the low flat forms of factories, past the statue of Lafayette on horseback, past the smokestacks black against a less-black sky, past the river, to where the hills glowed with the light from hundreds of three-deckers: glowing as they always had. I tried to imagine all the lives that had taken place inside those tenements, and all the lives that were still taking place there, behind those yellow-lit panes. A cab drove past, spraying mist from its tires and stirring the wet trash that stuck to the pavement; its tail-lights left a red trail in the street. I took Tommy by the arm. "Let's go back inside," I said.

I told an Irish joke. I thanked Barry Minkow and said what a pleasure it had been to work for him. I said what a great and honest mayor Tommy Lynch had been. I said how much I loved Mary, and what a blessed and fortunate life we'd had. Then I put a hand to my eyes and pretended to be choked up. "I'm sorry," I said. "I guess that's all I can manage."